Souls and Secrets

Portrait of Joseph Patai by Miklós Szines-Sternberg, September 1924.

SOULS AND SECRETS

Hasidic Stories

Joseph Patai

translated and with an introduction by Raphael Patai

illustrated by Miklós Szines-Sternberg

JASON ARONSON INC.
Northvale, New Jersey
London

This book was set in 13 pt. Berkeley Old Style by Alpha Graphics of Pittsfield, New Hampshire, and printed by Haddon Craftsmen in Scranton, Pennsylvania.

10 9 8 7 6 5 4 3 2 1

Library of Congress Cataloging-in-Publication Data

Patai, József, 1882-1953.
   [Short stories. English]
   Souls and secrets : Hasidic stories / by Joseph Patai ; translated and with an introduction by Raphael Patai ; illustrated by Miklós Szines-Sternberg.
     p. cm.
   ISBN 1-56821-355-7
   1. Short stories, Hungarian—Translations into English.
   2. Hasidim—Fiction. I. Patai, Raphael, 1910- . II. Title.
PH3291.P336A26   1995
894'.51133—dc20   94-45339

Manufactured in the United States of America. Jason Aronson Inc. offers books and cassettes. For information and catalog write to Jason Aronson Inc., 230 Livingston Street, Northvale, New Jersey 07647.

Contents

Introduction: Joseph Patai and
  His Hasidic Stories   vii

1 A Thousand and One Nights   1

2 The Old Psalmist   13

3 Queen Sabbath   27

4 The Mystery of the Bird's Nest   39

5 The Moon of the Tzaddik of Lublin   51

6 Struggle with the Evil One   59

7 The Booth of Rymanow   69

8 The Saint Who Loved to Sing   77

9 The Talmudist Maiden   89

10 The Death of the Baal Shem   99

11 The Tzaddik Who Craved the Messiah   109

12 The Prayer of the Flute   117

13 Mayerl   125

14 There Was Once a Dog   135

15 Story about the Story   143

16 The Etrog from the Holy Land   153

17 The Twelve Sabbath Breads   161

18 Velvele of Zbarazh   173

19 The Tzaddik Count   179

20 The Sons of Haman   187

21 The Great Conflict   197

22 The Cow of Reb Dovedl   205

23 Good-bye to the Booth   213

24 Three Bursts of Laughter   219

25 God, If You Had a Flock . . .   225

——Introduction——

Joseph Patai and His Hasidic Stories

y father, Joseph Patai (1882-1953), was a Hebrew and Hungarian poet, author, literary historian, editor, lecturer, and Zionist leader. But above everything else he was for more than three decades the foremost exponent, representative, and propagator of Jewish culture in Hungary. He taught me a lot, and I remember many of his pithy sayings, but none of them was as characteristic of his attitude to Judaism, Jewry, and Jewish culture than his oft-reiterated dictum: "One must force Jewish culture upon the Jews with fire and iron!" In saying this he had in mind primarily the Hungarian Jews, who were his flock, but as his travels made him acquainted with the Jews of other countries, he increasingly became aware of the lack of Jewish culture among them as well. He was convinced that instilling—if need be, "with fire and iron"—Jewish culture

into the Jews was the only way of insuring the survival of
the Jewish people, which for him was the greatest and
holiest commandment, to whose fulfillment he dedicated
his life.

He was a convinced and enthusiastic Zionist in a country where the Jewish establishment, the rabbinical leadership, and almost the entire Jewish community were not
only anti-Zionists but considered Zionism an unpatriotic
movement, and the Zionists disloyal to the Hungarian
homeland. But for Father, Zionism was not a political issue.
His love of the new *Eretz Yisrael* was based on his convic-
tion that the Hebrew culture that was being produced there
was a veritable lifesaver for the Jewish people all over the
Diaspora, and he devoted most of his work in Hungary to
writing and speaking about the new Hebrew literature, the
arts, the scholarly work, the economic and social experi-
mentation that were taking place in the renascent Jewish
Palestine.

One must remember that until the rise of Hitler, and in
many places even for several years after it, nobody in his
sane mind could have imagined that a time might come
when the existence of the Jews in the countries in which
they had lived for many centuries could be threatened, and
when Palestine would actually become a haven and refuge for the Jews of Europe. This was beyond the ken of
my father as well. But what he did observe, and what dis-
quieted him deeply, was the depletion made in the ranks
of Hungarian Jewry by conversion, intermarriage, and simply nonparticipation in Jewish life, as a result of which the
actual number of Budapest Jewry—close to a quarter mil-
lion in the first few years after World War I—alarmingly
diminished in the interwar years. And he was convinced

that only Jewish culture could provide the remedy and the prophylaxis against further spread of the erosion. He *knew* that once a Jew became imbued with a love and appreciation of Jewish culture he was protected against assimilation, and he felt that his life's mission was to present the Jews with the culture they had produced in the course of their long history, and were now renewing in their ancestral land, in its full beauty, so as to make it simply irresistible to them.

Even though Joseph Patai was a master of Hungarian poetry and prose, Hungarian was not his mother tongue, but the third language he acquired. Born in the village of Pata (full name: Gyöngyöspata), he was the oldest son of Reb Moshe Klein, who eked out a living as the village grocer but lived the intensely religious-emotional life of a true Hasid. The grocery was tended more often by his mother than by his father, who spent most of his time in the family room behind the store studying the Talmud and the *Zohar*. The language spoken in the family was Yiddish, and thus Yiddish was also Father's mother tongue. At the tender age of three his father began teaching him the Hebrew alphabet so as to enable him to read and understand the prayers and the Bible. At the age of four he was sent to the local *heder*, the elementary Jewish school, where he was taught *Humash* (the Five Books of Moses) with Rashi, and at the age of six was started on the *Bava Metzia* (Middle Gate) tractate of the Talmud. His parents knew Hungarian as well—they had to know, since their livelihood depended on contact with the local peasants who were the customers of their grocery—and thus little Yosele too acquired a smattering of Hungarian. At the age of six, in obedience to the laws of the country, he was sent to the

elementary school of Pata and thus brought his knowledge
of Hungarian up to the level of the other village children.
Because of this compulsory school attendance his studies
at the *heder* had to be confined to the afternoons, and thus
he went on studying in two schools simultaneously for four
years, from the age of six to ten.

When Father was in his eleventh year, Grandfather felt
that there was nothing more that the local *melammed*
(teacher) could teach him, and sent him to the yeshivah
of Kisvárda. Subsequently he became a student at five more
yeshivot one after the other: those of Sátoraljaujhely, Huszt,
Szatmár, Galgócz, and Nyitra. While in Nyitra he took the
step that once and for all removed him from the traditional
ultra-Orthodox hasidic world for which his father had intended him and enabled him to strike out in the direction
that he was to follow throughout his life: he left the yeshivah and entered the Roman Catholic *gimnázium* (high
school) maintained in that town by the Piarist Teaching
Order. When his father learned about this fatal step taken
by his eldest son, he considered him as having become
an apostate, as having died, and "sat *shivah*" over him, that
is, performed the traditional mourning ritual that required
sitting on the floor for seven days. Not until my father
married my mother, the daughter of a respected Orthodox Jew and descendant of the illustrious Sofer-Schreiber
rabbinical dynasty, was a reconciliation effected between
him and his implacable father.

Having finished the eight-year curriculum of the Piarist
high school in three years, Father earned his *matura* (high-
school certificate) and set out for Budapest, the Mecca of
all Hungarian Jewish youths with literary ambitions. He
studied for a while at the Budapest Rabbinical Seminary,

and then matriculated at the Budapest University. It was during his first few years in Budapest that he began to write. What the firstfruits of his literary efforts were is unknown, but they must have been Hebrew poetry, for his earliest surviving published writings consist of a slender volume (80 pages) of Hebrew poems titled *Shaashu'ei Alumim* (Delights of Youth), printed in Budapest in 1903. It contains original poems on biblical themes, lyrical poems, aphorisms, and translations into Hebrew of classical Hungarian poets. Thereafter almost fifty years had to pass before Father again wrote and published Hebrew poems, in his old age, after settling in Jerusalem.

By the time his Hebrew volume was published Father had embarked upon writing Hungarian poetry and soon became known as a promising young Hungarian Jewish poet. In 1904 the Israelite Congregation of Pest planned to enhance its Sabbath and holiday services in its great Dohány Street synagogue, as well as in the many other synagogues it maintained all over the city, by having Hungarian Jewish religious poems set to music recited alternatingly with the traditional Hebrew prayers. The fact that Chief Rabbi Samuel Kohn asked Father to provide the poems the congregation was looking for shows that by that time the twenty-two-year-old Joseph Patai (he had only recently Magyarized his name from Klein to Patai) was recognized as the foremost Hungarian Jewish poet or at least as one of the most outstanding such poets. Father's poems were actually incorporated into the synagogal liturgy, and they were also published under the title *Templomi énekek* (Temple Songs).

From the same years dates Father's commitment to Zionism. In 1903 he was among the handful of university students who founded the students' organization *Mak-kabea*, which was to develop into the hub of Zionist work in Hungary, even though the Zionist movement as a whole was to remain rudimentary in the country until the very days of the Holocaust.

Also in the early 1900s, Father was asked by Miksa Szabolcsi, editor-in-chief of *Egyenlőség* (Equality), the fore-most Jewish weekly in Budapest, to join his editorial staff. It was from Szabolcsi that Father acquired the art of jour-nalism, which he fully recognized by using for years the pen name "Secundus," implying that Miksa Szabolcsi was the "primus" of the guild. At the same time Father contin-ued and concluded his university studies and in 1907 was awarded the doctorate and the year thereafter, the high-school teacher's certificate in Hungarian and German lit-erature. Still in 1908 he became a substitute, and in 1910 a regular, teacher of these subjects at the Budapest Inner City High School of which Theodor Herzl had been a stu-dent in the years 1870–1877. This appointment enabled him to resign from *Egyenlőség,* in which he felt increasingly uncomfortable due to its outspoken anti-Zionist position.

At the same time Father began to work on translating into Hungarian the great medieval Hebrew poets, and in 1905 he published a volume containing the first of these translations as the third in a modest series of books he started to edit under the title *Magyar Zsidó Könyvtár* (Hun-garian Jewish Library). This series of books, and especially his fine translations, established his reputation as an out-standing young Hungarian Jewish poet, editor, and cul-tural activist. In that early period of his life (he was alto-gether 23 years old!) work for Jewish culture did not yet absorb all his interests and energies. He had strongly socialistic inclinations as manifested, for instance, in several poems on a powerfully revolutionary note he published in the leading Budapest Socialist paper *Népszava* (The People's Voice) in that very year of 1905.

However, Judaism and Jewishness were already his overwhelming preoccupations at that time. In 1906 he published a large volume of poems, titled *Babylon Vizein* (On the Waters of Babylon), which contains poems of a deeply Jewish character, the like of which had never before been written in the Hungarian language. By that time Father had met Mother, and a friendship and a community of interests had developed between them, as evidenced by an illustration, a pen drawing contained in *Babylon Vizein* and signed E. Ehrenfeld, Mother's maiden family name with the initial of her first name, Edith.

Father's courtship, as was not unusual in those days, was a long and patient one, and it was not until 1909, after he got his high-school appointment, that they married. By a lucky coincidence, Father was awarded at the same time a generous stipend from the Hungarian Ministry of Culture to enable him to go to England, and in particular to Oxford, to study at the Bodleian Library the unpublished Hebrew poets of past centuries. He intended to publish their poetry in a Hungarian translation as a continuation of the work he had begun a few years earlier. Stopping over for several days in London, my parents lodged with the editor of a British Jewish yearbook, and when Father got acquainted with the work of his host, he conceived of the idea of publishing a Hungarian Jewish almanac devoted to Jewish culture, art, literature, and social affairs. For the capital that had to be invested in this venture, my parents, at my mother's suggestion, used the dowry that she had received from her well-to-do maternal grandmother, the widow of Raphael Kurländer of Nagyvárad, the erstwhile president of the Orthodox Jewish community of that Transylvanian city. Her father was a rabbinical scholar who made only a very modest living as the Budapest representative of a Debrecen brush factory. Thus came into being the magnificent, large-sized, and beautifully produced volume titled *Magyar Zsidó Almanach* (Hungarian Jewish Almanac, Budapest, 1911), which was not only a great literary success, but—mirabile dictu!—yielded an unexpectedly high financial return as well. With its appearance, the twenty-eight-year-old Joseph Patai became a leading personality on the Hungarian Jewish cultural scene.

As for the Patais' private family scene, it became enriched by my appearance in November 1910, making the young couple feel that life was good to them and that they had achieved much of what they could aspire to. They called me in Hungarian Ervin György, and in Hebrew, after my mother's recently deceased grandfather, Raphael.

The success of the *Almanach* encouraged my parents to turn it into a permanent venture. They transformed it into a monthly devoted to Jewish literature, art, culture, and society, called it *Mult és Jövő* (Past and Future), and identified it as volume two of the *Hungarian Jewish Almanac*. Thereafter, until my parents left Budapest for Palestine in the fall of 1939, my father's main work consisted of editing this journal and taking care of such other affairs as grew out of publishing it. Within a year or so after launching his journal, Father had become recognized as the foremost Jewish cultural leader in Hungary and the main representative in the Hungarian Jewish community of the new

Hebrew culture that was developing by leaps and bounds in *Eretz Yisrael*.

Father's busy life embraced many other activities as well. First of all, until 1919 he filled a full-time position as teacher of Hungarian and German literature in the city high school. In that year he went into early retirement to be able to devote himself fully to his literary, editorial, and cultural work. Although there was no dearth of literary contributions furnished by Hungarian Jewish writers to his journal, still a considerable part of the material published in its forty pages month after month was written by him. It was in *Mult és Jövő* that he first published his original poems, his translations of Hebrew poets, his short stories (of them more below), his descriptions of his travels in the "Holy Land," his articles in many of which he castigated the leadership of the Israelite Congregation of Pest, his programmatical papers in which he instructed the Jews of Hungary in what they were duty-bound to do, his ironical comments on Hungarian Jewish and non-Jewish life as he observed it, and many other types of writings. At the same time he wrote and published (under the aegis of *Mult és Jövő*) a series of books of Jewish interest: a book of memoirs about his childhood in Pata, a biography of Theodor Herzl, a Palestinian travelogue, a five-volume anthology of Hebrew poets in his own Hungarian translation, books of his own poetry, volumes of essays on the general theme of "Fight for Jewish Culture," an art book containing reproductions of paintings by the world's greatest masters illustrating the Bible, and more and more.

As his popularity grew, so did the number of invitations he received from the Jewish communities in Hungary and in the Hungarian-speaking detached territories to come and lecture, mostly on Hebrew poetry and literature, on Jewish culture, and on the renascent Holy Land. Many times several congregations within an area joined together and invited him to lecture tours. My impression is that for many years he must have given no fewer than about twenty-five to thirty lectures annually outside Budapest and several more in the capital itself.

Every year in Budapest he organized one or two cultural evenings in which the foremost Hungarian (Jewish and non-Jewish) performing artists—actors, singers, musicians—presented Jewish poetry, belles lettres, songs, and music. Usually he himself introduced the evening with an impressive address, always enthusiastically received by the audience. Invariably, even the largest concert halls in which these events took place were filled to capacity. Several times Father invited to these cultural evenings one or the other of the best-known Jewish and Palestinian Hebrew poets and authors, whose personal appearances were added attractions for the Budapest Jews and whose works, in Father's Hungarian translation, were presented by famous actors of the Hungarian stage. He also organized picture exhibitions for recognized Jewish artists from abroad, including some who lived in *Eretz Yisrael*, and in this manner made Jewish art in general, and Palestinian Jewish arts in particular, known and appreciated in Hungary. And last but not least, the conducted tours he led every spring to Palestine gave an opportunity to many Hungarian Jews to get a firsthand glimpse of the *Yishuv*, and, incidentally, to some to remain illegally in Palestine and augment the numbers of *Aliyah Bet*. As this brief, and incomplete, enumeration shows, Father more than deserved the designa-

tion his adherents and admirers gave him, "the Ambassa-
dor of Jewish Culture in Hungary."

Lest the foregoing sketch create the impression that
Joseph Patai's work was totally confined to propagating
Jewish culture within the Jewish community of Hungary,
I want to mention two more arenas of his activities not
touched upon hitherto. Both demonstrate that, when he
felt it necessary, he did not hesitate to enter into the thick-
ets of inter-Jewish politics and that he knew how to make
Jewish community politics the maidservant of Jewish culture. In 1919, after the fall of the Communist regime,
Hungary was in the grip of the so-called White Terror, and
the position of the entire Jewish community in the country was endangered. In that situation Patai felt that politics remained the only weapon left to the Jews, and in its
service he launched a political weekly that he titled *The
Weekly of Mult és Jövő*. He published this weekly for close
to three years, and with it he fought for Jewish interests
and against every individual, group, party, trend, and movement, whether Jewish or gentile, that he considered a danger for Jewish survival in Hungary. In this weekly too, as
in his monthly, much of the material published stemmed
from his own pen, and how fearless he was in his fight is
shown by the frequent blank spaces that indicate the hand
of the censor, who found much of what Patai wrote un-
palatable from the point of view of the regime.

About 1925 Patai became convinced that, given the
Hungarian patriotic imperative that dominated Jewish
sentiments, political Zionism, as represented by the Hungarian Zionist Federation, had no hope of gaining the
support of either the leading element of Hungarian Jewry
or of broad segments of the Jewish community. In search-

ing for a way to remedy this situation, Patai conceived of the same idea that, a few years later (in 1929 to be precise), Chaim Weizmann introduced into the World Zionist Organization: to set up an organizational framework that would enable non-Zionists to participate together with Zionists in supporting the cultural, social, and economic (that is, nonpolitical) activities of the *Yishuv*. He was able to persuade several non-Zionist leading personalities of Hungarian Jewry to join him in founding the Pro Palestine Association of Hungarian Jews, under whose aegis, from 1926 on, most of the Hungarian Jewish "Palestine work" was carried out.

Because of the importance of his cultural embassy, which did not cease even after the introduction of the infamous Hungarian Jewish laws of 1938 and 1939 (*Mult és Jövő* remained the only Jewish journal not suspended), Father just could not bring himself to leave Hungary and make his *aliyah* to *Eretz Yisrael*, even after the outbreak of World War II and despite the fact that by that time all three of his children had settled in Palestine. In the summer of 1939 my sister Eva and I were in Paris, and as soon as the war broke out we hurried back to Palestine. Because of the difficulties in Mediterranean shipping, we had to wait for several days in Trieste until a ship finally sailed for Haifa. We made use of our forced stopover to phone every evening to our parents in Budapest; I tried to make use of all the arguments I could think of to persuade Father to leave while it was still possible; my sister cried and carried on over the phone and had veritable hysterical seizures, screaming that unless they left right away she knew she would never again see her parents. These arguments finally had their effect, and our parents left Budapest for Trieste, where they were able to board the last ship that sailed for Haifa before war conditions closed down that one remaining outlet from Hungary to the free world. Father lived for another fourteen years in Palestine; Mother survived him by twenty-three years. What he wrote, did, and experienced in that closing phase of his life in Palestine is another chapter that does not belong in this context.

Most of the Hasidic stories published here were written by Father between 1910 and 1920. A few more he added in the 1920s. He published the original edition, containing sixteen stories, in 1918, with this dedication: "To My Mother, the Dame Shoshanna-Hayla, who put me to sleep and kept me awake with her sacred stories." *Dame* is the best I can do in trying to translate into English the Hungarian honorific title *nagyasszony*, literally "great woman," by which my father refers to his mother, who had, as I know from what Father told me on the rare occasions that he spoke to me in his old age about his parents, an exceptional command of the vast storehouses of popular Yiddish literature that constituted the traditional culture of pious East European Jewish women down to the twentieth century.

But of course, even if he heard the gist of several of these stories from his mother, what Father did with that raw material was to cast it into a highly artistic format and endow it with a warmth, a psychological refinement, a dimension of sensitivity, and a characterization entirely lacking in their original versions. As Leo Singer, who translated these stories into German (see Josef Patai, *Kabala:*

Seelen und Welten. Berlin: Jüdischer Verlag, 1919), remarked in his introduction, "what became under his hands, e.g., of the beautiful, well-known motive of the *Shivhei haAri*, the reader of the 'Queen Sabbath' story can judge for himself."

Which leads me to a few comments of my own on Father's Hasidic stories in the light of, and in comparison to, the collections of Hasidic material available in English.

*   *   *

Let me begin by saying a few words on the Hasidic movement that in the late eighteenth and early nineteenth century threatened to split the East European Jewish community into two. The split probably would have occurred had it not been for the appearance of the *Haskalah*, the Jewish Enlightenment, which united the Hasidim and their opponents (the *mitnagdim*), both of whom felt threatened by the *Haskalah*'s unprecedented inroads into Jewish traditionalism.

Hasidism (also spelled Ḥasidism, Hassidism, Chasidism, Chassidism) is the name of the popular mystical-religious movement initiated by Rabbi Israel ben Eliezer (1700–1760), known as the "*Baal Shem Tov*," that is, "Master of the Good (Divine) Name," or perhaps "Good Master of the (Divine) Name," or by the acronym of these three words, "BeShT." Hasidism differed in many respects from traditional Orthodox Judaism, but primarily in its emphasis on the duty of serving God in joy. As the Tzaddik of Przemysl says in Joseph Patai's story "Mayerl" (story 13), "Sadness is the greatest sin. . . . The Shekhinah is present only where there is joy!" The same idea was expressed in a Hebrew folksong still popular in the *Yishuv* in the 1930s:

Lo atzevet, bahurim,	No sadness, good friends,
bahurim	good friends,
Harabbi tzivvah lismoah	The Rabbi commanded
	us to rejoice,
Kol hayyenu akhurim,	All our lives are troubled,
akhurim,	troubled,
Umitzvah hatzaar	And it is a *mitzvah* to
lishkoah	forget the pain . . . .

One of the most significant contributions Hasidism made to the enrichment of Jewish life in East Europe was the folktale. While the Besht was still alive, stories about him began to circulate in the rapidly growing communities of his followers. Soon his disciples started to collect them, and before long printed versions of *Shivhei haBeShT* (Praises of the BeShT) began to appear. Hasidism spread, and Hasidic *rebbes* (rabbis, masters, teachers) sprang up all over the Ukraine, Volhynia, Central Poland, Galicia, as far north as Belorussia, and as far south as Bukovina, Moldavia, and Hungary. Many of these *rebbes* attracted sizable communities that almost developed into independent sects. Tales and legends about these masters of the second and subsequent generations began to be told, and in turn to be collected and published. From the mid-nineteenth century on, hundreds of Hasidic story anthologies appeared, and soon thereafter they also began to be translated from the Hebrew originals into other languages. By 1934, Louis I. Newman and Samuel Spitz in their classic, *The Hasidic Anthology*, could list more than 120 sources they were able to utilize, and following it more and more collections of Hasidic stories saw the light of day. These collections inevitably attracted scholarly attention, and thus a new area of research within Jewish studies, that of Hasidic folk literature, developed. The publication of anthologies in Hebrew and in English continued unabated. In the year 1993 alone, one single American publisher, Jason Aronson Inc., published no fewer than four volumes of Hasidic tales (*In Praise of the Baal Shem Tov*, by Dan Ben-Amos and Jerome R. Mintz; *Why the Baal Shem Tov Laughed*, by Sterna Citron; *Nine Gates to the Chasidic Mysteries*, by Jiri Langer; and *The Prince Who Turned into a Rooster*, by Tzvi Rabinowicz). It is evident that interest in the Hasidic tale has not diminished as Hasidism itself enters the third century of its existence.

Hungary lay on the southwestern outskirts of the Hasidic diffusion. By the late nineteenth century she could boast of a few Hasidic dynasties, each with its "court" and fervent followers. But it was not until the interwar years that one Hungarian master, the Satmarer *Rov*, whose city by that time had been incorporated into Rumania, achieved a name, a fame, and a following approaching, and even exceeding, those of the earlier *rebbes* of the lands farther to the north. Other Hungarian Hasidic centers were Sátoraljaujhely (Ohel), Munkács (Mukachevo), and Máramaros-Sziget (Sighet). From these cities Hasidism spread to other parts of northern Hungary, including the capital, Budapest.

The village of Pata, where my paternal grandmother and my father were born, lies some ninety miles to the southwest of Sátoraljaujhely, the nearest significant Hasidic center. During my father's childhood, Grandfather seems to have been a Hasid of the Rebbe of Belz. I have reason to assume that he periodically visited that great Hasidic center to the north of the Carpathians on the border between Poland and the Ukraine, but later he switched allegiance and became an adherent of the "Satmarer." In 1920, when the anti-Semitic wave that swept Hungary following the ouster of the short-lived Communist regime reached Pata, and Grandfather's store was attacked and looted, he and Grandmother moved from Pata to Satmar. Grandfather evidently chose to move there in order to be near his *rebbe*. As for Father, although in his adolescence he turned irreligious and then became an apostle of Jewish culture, he never ceased to be emotionally attached to the Hasidism he had absorbed in his childhood from the precept and example of his father and, perhaps even more so, from the tales he later termed "sacred stories," told him by his mother.

Once he found his footing in Hungarian letters and embarked upon his lifelong mission of instilling Jewish culture into the largely assimilant Hungarian Jewish community, it was almost inevitable that Father should consider the beauty hidden in the Hasidic tale a value he wanted to present to his readership. But in order to do so he had first to recast those tales into a truly artistic form, to endow them with a content and a significance beyond what they possessed in their original versions in which they were in most cases brief, fragmentary, and of a didactic intent. By that time, of course, he could draw not merely on what he remembered from his mother's stories, but on his wide reading of the available Hasidic literature. Taking those stories, or story fragments, as the basis, he created highly artistic short stories, each one of which is a gem encapsulating a shining moment in Hasidic life. What demonstrates most clearly the indelible influence the Hasi-

dic world had on my father is that while his writings include a great variety of genres—as shown above, he wrote
poetry, biography, feuilletons, political articles, criticism,
polemics, and other types of letters—Hasidic tales were the
only prose fiction he ever wrote, making a modest total of
twenty-five stories.

A modest total, but of what quality! Each of them is
suffused with a deep love of the Hasidic world, the simple
Hasidic believer, and, above all, the Tzaddik, the Hasidic
master. The average run-of-the-mill Hasidim of his stories,
who form the background against which his protagonist,
the Tzaddik, appears as a being of an altogether higher
order, are rather humble, simpleminded persons, who
believe, obey, and live entirely within the world of the
mitzvot, the religious commandments. They do not understand the deeper and at the same time higher meaning of
the *mitzvot,* which demands of the believers a degree of
spirituality they alone, without the guidance of their saintly
leader and master, are not capable of achieving. But, nevertheless, they are lovable people, most of whom live in
poverty, but all of whom have an irrepressible hankering
after the higher world of which their Tzaddik is the earthly
representative.

Beyond the variety of the actual events described in the
stories, there is one great common theme: the Tzaddik's
understanding of true values, of true religiosity, of true
piety, of the true way of fulfilling what the Holy One,
blessed be He, wants of man. Acts that the average believer
thinks are sinful can turn out, when the Tzaddik reveals
their true meaning, to be expressions of a higher piety.
How a seemingly sinful act can have a greater and higher
hidden value is beautifully illustrated in several stories,

such as those about the ignorant boy's playing his flute on Yom Kippur (story 12), the poor man's placing twelve Sabbath breads into the Holy Ark (story 17), and the gentile shepherd's drinking the sacred wine of the cup of Elijah on the *Seder* table (story 8). Others of the stories show that simple piety, even the most simpleminded reliance on the Holy One, blessed be He, is dearer to God than the most meticulous observance of the minutiae of the Law and the luxurious indulgence in performing complex religious ceremonies (story 2).

Several of the stories contained in this book show what Joseph Patai's art was able to do with the simplest motives or fragments of Hasidic tales. Take, for instance, the image of the saintly Mayerl, the Tzaddik of Przemysl, about whom he wrote one of his most prepossessing and charming stories. The traditional kernel of that story is given in Jiri Langer's *Nine Gates of the Chasidic Mysteries* (p. 62), where it reads in bland and pale brevity:

> Most of all Mayerl preferred to pray for the really bad sinners, to obtain God's forgiveness for them. And indeed, God always pardoned them immediately when he interceded for them. But once—it only happened once, of course, only one single time—when Mayerl interceded for a particularly hardened and shameful sinner, and God this time simply would not forgive, then Mayerl—just think of it!—actually stamped his foot at God. And the man was immediately pardoned.

Now read the full, vibrant, and heartwarming story (story 13) Father tells of Mayerl, the totally unselfish, saintly Hasidic master, whose relationship to God is that of a pampered child to his loving father, who is secure in his knowledge that his Heavenly Father will always do what he requests of Him, who rejoices when he loses his own "share in the World to Come" because of his promise of a place in Paradise to an inveterate sinner, and Heaven above always must fulfill what Mayerl promises down here on earth. I don't know from what source Father took the kernel for this story. It could not be R. Margulies's *Or haMeir*, quoted by Louis I. Newman in his *Hasidic Anthology* (p. 417), because that booklet was published in 1926, after Father wrote his own story. But whatever the source, it is evident that not more than a very minor part of the story is taken from it, and the full richness of the narrative, with its loving characterization of the happy-go-lucky, but at the same time totally self-denying saint, its presentation of the image of Mayerl with his naive, almost childish, relationship to God and his limitless trust in the love, protection, and forgiveness of his Heavenly Father—all this is the product of Joseph Patai's poetic imagination, of his vision of the ideal Hasidic master. We feel that Joseph Patai loved Mayerl at least as much as Mayerl loved God and His creatures.

The same relationship between source material and the fully developed form of the narrative characterizes all the Hasidic stories written by Joseph Patai. One more example will have to suffice. The story of "The Three Laughters" (story 24) is one of the better-known Hasidic tales, appearing both in Sterna Citron's *Why the Baal Shem Laughed* (pp. 3-5), and Tzvi Rabinowicz's *The Prince Who Turned into a Rooster* (pp. 26-30). In both these versions the Tzaddik around whom the story revolves is the Baal Shem Tov, who is endowed with the power of seeing what happens in distant places; he laughs three times because he sees that the poor bookbinder Shabsei of the village of Opatow (thus in Rabinowicz) or Reb Shabsai of Koznitz (according to Citron) dances in joy three times with his wife. The occasion for those three dances? The poor couple has no money to buy food for the Sabbath, and the bookbinder is ready to spend the Sabbath in fasting, but his wife, while cleaning the house for the Sabbath, finds some silver buttons, or some long-lost jewelry, which she quickly sells and thus is able to buy food and prepare a Sabbath meal. When Shabsei/Shabsai comes home from the synagogue Friday night, and finds the rich Sabbath meal waiting for him and learns what happened, in his joy he gets hold of his wife and dances with her around the table three times. This is what the Tzaddik sees from the distance, and this is what makes him laugh three times.

In my father's version the Tzaddik who laughs three times is the Tzaddik of Nemirov. The man who dances three times with his wife is the tailor Mendele, who lives in the same place. What his wife finds is her long-lost engagement ring. Much more significant, however, than these differences in concrete detail is the framing of the story itself, and the significance given to it. In both the Citron and Rabinowicz versions the story revolves around the three laughters of the Tzaddik, which in the sequence are explained by his having seen the poor man dancing with his wife: that distant sight made the heart of the Tzaddik merry. This is all: the poverty-stricken couple finds a long-lost piece of jewelry, which enables them to buy food for the Sabbath, they dance in merriment, the Tzaddik sees it and laughs. The story has no moral significance, it is the simple story of a lucky break, the joyous reaction of the poor couple, and the Tzaddik's laughter upon seeing it.

In my father's version the incident of the three laughters is placed against the background of describing, to begin with, the habitual seriousness and dignity of the Nemirover Tzaddik. On the Friday night in question he was even more than usually somber and subdued, had an extremely worried mien, and the believers, observing him, were afraid that he may be concerned about something very weighty, perhaps fateful. But nobody dared to ask him what preoccupied him. It was at that point that the Tzaddik was seized by the three unexpected and inexplicable spasms of laughter. Their true meaning becomes clear only next evening, after the outgoing of the Sabbath, when the Tzaddik asks Mendele, the poor old tailor, who modestly sits at the far end of the Tzaddik's table, what he did on Friday night. Mendele shamefacedly tells the Tzaddik and his followers about his dancing with his wife, and the Tzaddik explains to the believers what chain of events was triggered by that spontaneous outburst of joy by the poverty-stricken old couple: the heavenly Accuser had brought terrible charges against Israel, even the Shekhinah had looked down on earth with wrath, and the Children of Israel were in grave danger. But when the Shekhinah noticed the old couple dance in their innocent joy, she "smiled three times, and those three smiles decided the fate of the Children of Israel." In this manner the old couple's dancing becomes endowed with a weighty, mystical, fateful significance that lifts it out of the trivial and makes it into an unsuspected but important link in a chain of cosmic events, in a sequence of heavenly happenings. The Tzaddik's laughter, too, we now understand, was not merely merriment over the happy prancing of a poverty-stricken old couple, but the expression of his immense relief at seeing that such a little act of innocent gaiety by poor and pious old Mendele and his wife was able to tilt the balance in favor of the succor of Israel. In a word, under Joseph Patai's masterly hand the insignificant little story has become transformed into an account of a mystical Hasidic experience of great moment.

Joseph Patai in his Hasidic stories took traditional Hasidic tales as the kernel and built upon them fully developed genre pictures of Hasidic life, including in most of them the account of some unusual event that shook a Hasidic community and showed how a puzzling occurrence was explained by the Tzaddik, the admired and adored spiritual leader of the believers. Patai's Tzaddik is a miracle-working saint, but his miracles consist not of performing acts or producing phenomena that are contrary to the physical laws of nature, but are psychological marvels that appear miraculous because they manifest a "miraculous" understanding of human nature and of divine law, of the ways of man and of God, and open up unsuspected spiritual dimensions to the trusting eyes and minds of the simple followers.

The traditional Hasidic tale in its original form is extremely short, in fact so short as to be frequently splintered and fragmentary. The most complete collection of Hasidic tales available in English, Louis I. Newman's classic *Hasidic Anthology*, for example, contains in its 531 text pages more than 3,000 tale fragments (culled from 121 Hebrew and Yiddish sources), or almost 6 items per page. Likewise, Dan Ben-Amos and Jerome R. Mintz's scholarly *In Praise of the Baal Shem Tov* has in its 261 text pages 251 stories, or about one story per page. As these examples show, the traditional Hasidic tale is a narrative art form

not characterized by a building up of character, an offering of detailed description, and a development of plot or
story line, but rather by a hurried presentation of a frac-
tional, isolated item, without connection to antecedent,
context, and environment.

This, then, was the kind of rudimentary raw material that
stood at the disposal of Joseph Patai when he wrote his
Hasidic stories. He found, either in the recesses of his
childhood memories or in the treasure troves of the
Hasidic literature he read in later years nothing more than
brief fragments of stories told in a few throw-away lines,
but they were sufficient to set off the creative process in
his mind and to build around them finely structured and
carefully balanced complete stories in which the interac-
tion between the Tzaddik and the believers is carefully
developed from the initial clash to the ultimate resolution.
With a deep poetic empathy he created characters, he provided them with an environment and a society which they
needed to be able to live and breathe, he invented and described events and put dialogue into the mouths of pro-
tagonists that brought them to life, produced tensions
among them, and inevitably made the reader want to know
what happened next. In a word, his Hasidic stories are
entirely Joseph Patai's own creations, as much his as, say,
Robert Graves's *I, Claudius* is his, despite any historical
sources he utilized in creating it. And yet, what Joseph Patai
achieved by writing his Hasidic stories, and by showing
Hasidic life with love and in a garb of beauty, was to make
the world of the Hasidim known to a wide Hungarian Jewish readership and to bring close to it, and make it admire,
a type of Jewish life of which it had been either contemp-
tuous as "Galician" superstition, or, in most cases, totally

ignorant. He showed that Hasidism was a precious part of the rich and many-faceted Jewish culture.

This, in ultimate analysis, is what distinguishes Joseph Patai's Hasidic stories: they allow the reader to get a whiff of the spiritual quality that suffused Hasidic life and make him sense the added dimension, over and above those of space and time, in which the Hasidim lived. They enable him to get a taste of what it meant to be endowed with the absolute certainty that God kept His loving eye upon you and that you could always know what He wanted of you because the Tzaddik was there to teach you and guide you.

*   *   *

In conclusion, a word about the illustrator. All I was able to ascertain about Miklós Szines-Sternberg was that he was born in Hungary, in 1901, studied in Budapest at the College of Fine Arts and also with the highly respected painter Gustáv Magyar-Mannheimer, and was still in Budapest in 1924. At that time he drew a pencil portrait (at present in my possession) of the Hebrew poet Saul Tchernichovsky in my parents' house, where the latter stayed as a guest on the occasion of his appearance at a cultural evening Father organized in his honor. It must have been in that year that the artist drew some three dozen charcoal drawings illustrating my father's Hasidic stories. These drawings remained the property of my father, and after his death we his three children divided them among us. At present, they are partly in my possession, partly in the possession of my brother Saul in Jerusalem, and partly in the possession of my niece Mira Zakkai, in Givatayim, Israel. In 1925, Miklós Szines-Sternberg moved to Paris, where he became known as an illustrator under the name

Nicolas Sternberg. Among his works was the illustrated edition of Jules Barbey d'Aurevilly's chef-d'oeuvre, the collection *Les Diaboliques*, which was first published in 1874. (See Ármin Beregi, "Szines-Sternberg Miklós útja Párisig" ["The Road of Miklós Szines-Sternberg to Paris"], *Mult és Jövő* 16:174-75, Budapest, 1926.) In 1929 he had an exhibition at the Galeries Georges Petit (8, rue de Séze, Paris), in which 173 of his drawings were presented, including 40 that illustrated the mystical world of the Kabbala, and others inspired by the Hebrew theater Habimah. In volume 20 (1930) of the illustrated journal *L'Art et les Artistes* the critic André Warnod published an article about him in which he spoke of him as of an artist of the highest merits. His work received accolades also in the general press, including *Paris-Soir*, in which Paul Reboux called him "A Mozart of the crayon," who from the age of six "created compositions surprising in their richness of exactitude, of proportion, of the expression of physiognomies . . ." Yvan Noé in *L'Ami du Peuple* wrote that "Sternberg's talent is on the margins of contemporary painting; his art is direct, robust, tormented, inquiet, universal, animated by a quasi-mystical passion that wants to embrace simultaneously all forms of sensibility . . ." His biography is contained in the *Allgemeines Lexikon der bildenden Künste*, volume 32, Leipzig, 1938.

Raphael Patai
Forest Hills, New York

Cover picture prepared by Miklós Szines-Sternberg in 1924 for the illustrated
edition of Joseph Patai's Hasidic stories. The edition was published in 1935,
but this picture was not used. The inscription at the top of the picture reads
(in Hungarian): "Szines's Visions to the Patai KABBALA." The head is a styl-
ized self-portrait of the artist.

—1—

A Thousand
and One Nights

hen the idea was born in the heart of the Saint of Belz to build a vast new Hall for the Divine Matron who was wandering in Exile, he timidly went to his beautiful spouse and with a sorrowful face said to her:

"Rachel, I shall have to stay awake a thousand nights, so that my soul can delve for a thousand midnight hours into the Mystery of Mysteries, that through a thousand nights I immerse myself in the Sea of Secrets whose sparkling waters purify the heart and whose radiance shows dazzling heavens to the eye. For a thousand nights we must separate, so that the secret of building a Temple be revealed to my soul."

Rachel cast down her eyes and said sadly:

"Rabbi, until now I have never left you. Like a faithful shadow I followed you on all your ways, and you often told me that you would take me along even into the Halls

1

of Heaven. When your soul submerged into the Sea of Deep Mysteries, when your prayer winged its way to the heights of Heaven, I always stood there before your door, and watched the quiver of your eyes, the tremor of your lips. I rejoiced in your joy and suffered with your suffering. If you have to stay awake a thousand nights, let me hold the candle over your table, allow me to light up your holy books."

The Tzaddik thought for a moment, and then, looking into the pale face of Rachel, said tenderly:

"You are so weak, my soul, you should rest. I am afraid you could not endure it. As for me, I am sustained by the yearning, kept awake by the hunger for the Mystery of Mysteries, but you would only become more enfeebled by the vigil."

"Oh, reveal then to me too the Mystery of Mysteries! Have you not said many times that our souls are one? That which kindles the light of lights in your soul will perhaps dispel also the darkness of my soul."

"Rachel, do not ask this," begged the Tzaddik in an almost beseeching tone. "My soul, do not lead me into temptation. Rather keep vigil next to me through a thousand nights, but do not ask this of me. Perhaps its time too will come, beyond the thousand nights."

And the Tzaddik of Belz and his pale, white spouse, Rachel, kept vigil together in the Room of Books. The Tzaddik, clad in snow-white linen raiment, wrapped in a white satin cloak, sat at the table decked with a pure white cloth, his head, covered by a white velvet cap, bent over the large folio. And next to him, clothed in sparkling white silk, with a diadem of precious stones on her head, sat Rachel, holding two white candles in her white hands over the open book.

"They sit next to each other like bride and groom just come from under the wedding baldachin," said one of the believers, who passed by the Room of Books and cast a curious glance into it.

"Like Adam and Eve in the Garden of Eden, so pure and innocent are they," said another exuberantly.

"And Rachel, holding the candles, is saintly and sparkling like a golden candelabrum of the Holy Temple," raved a third one.

And Rachel kept vigil night after night. In the afternoon, when the Tzaddik took a little rest, she too rested. But toward evening, when the Tzaddik led the *Minhah* prayer, she already stood there in the doorway, gazed with delight at the transfigured countenance of the Tzaddik, watched his elated movements, imbibed the deep sighs that welled up from his breast and seemed to help the struggling supplications rise up to the high heavens. After the prayer the believers came with their thousand requests, each one with his own trouble, pain, misery. And Rachel stood there on the threshold and listened raptly to the words of the Tzaddik, how he comforted, how he encouraged, how he poured confidence into the dispirited, armed the feeble with strength, lifted up the desperate. And the Tzaddik would always look at Rachel as if he were expecting approval, encouragement from her eyes. And on such occasions their eyes would meet, and those to whom it was vouchsafed to see could see that from the meeting of their eyes a spark jumped out and rose up into the heights of Heaven like fire from a sacred altar, taking along all the requests of those stricken by fate.

When the Room of Requests finally emptied, the Tzaddik moved into the Room of Books, and Rachel, with two candles in her hands, followed him silently. The light of the candles cast a glow upon their faces. The forehead of the Tzaddik, bent over the folios, gathered into deeper and deeper wrinkles, as if the plow of mysteries had cut furrows into it. The face of Rachel became paler and paler, her eyes more feverish, more faint. Her hands too seemed to become more and more withered, more and more tremulous night after night. The tallow that melted from the candles dripped down on her fingers and burned red spots into them. But Rachel did not even notice it. Her soul tried to follow the ways of the Tzaddik's soul. She would have liked to soar with him, to fly with the wings of his thoughts. Perhaps she too could understand, perhaps to her too new heavens and new earths would open. In the Room of Requests she knew all the thoughts of the Tzaddik, there she could almost have uttered each of his words in advance, but here, in the Room of Books, she could move only gropingly, like a blind man in a hall lighted up with a myriad of sparkling lamps.

And Rachel looked with wistful, thirsty eyes at the Tzaddik.

"Rabbi," she suddenly blurted out, "open up before me too the Gates of Mysteries!"

The Tzaddik gave a start, raised his heavy lashes from the great folio, and looked at Rachel reproachfully, as if she had shooed away a wondrous colorful dream bird from him.

"You promised, Rachel," he said, "that you would ask no questions. Only a few nights remain until the thousandth night."

"Only a few nights," Rachel burst out, "only a few nights, and your beard, Rabbi, has become white like your cloak, and your white cap cannot be distinguished from the whiteness of your hair!"

"Do not continue," interrupted the Tzaddik. "I am compensated by the Sea of Mysteries, which rejuvenates the soul, a few drops of whose water make the wings of the soul grow so as to be able to soar up into the purity of the infinite azure. I am searching for the secret of building the Temple, and if I find it, I shall build a great new Temple, and the mourning Shekhinah, who wanders in Exile, will come here, and from the ruins of the Jerusalem Temple and until this place she will find nothing impure on her way. I am building a Temple for Redemption, but you, Rachel, why are your cheeks sunken? Why are your eyes so red? Go, Rachel, take a rest."

"And I can have no share in the building of the Temple? Am I not your helpful servant?"

"You uttered an ugly word, Rachel," reprimanded the Tzaddik. "You are not a servant, you are a queen! Yes, you are a queen, Rachel! And know, then, in this mysterious hour of Grace, that also the King of Kings needs His Queen, because without her his dominion is not complete."

The clock on the wall struck midnight. The Tzaddik stopped talking, listened to the hollow, sad strokes of the clock, and then continued as if speaking to himself:

"At this moment the Shekhinah, the Holy Bride, puts on all her jewelry, and the Bridegroom, enwreathed, sets forth to seek her out. At this moment, in the Above, there opens the Hall of Love, which is full of Mercy and contains the Secrets of Secrets. At this moment, in the infinite, the Father and the Mother embrace, the Sphere of Glory circles toward the Sphere of the Queen, the Earth yearns for Heaven, the Sun seeks the Moon, the Material pines for the Form, and the Soul, that exiled gazelle, seeks thirstily her old spring. New worlds are being created in the Mysteries of the Kisses, and happy are they who become intoxicated with the bliss of such kisses."

Rachel drank in rapturously the words of the Tzaddik, bent down over him and almost touched him with her lips, but drew back lest she drive away the long-waited moment.

"And did the Groom find his Bride?" she asked in a whisper, dreamily.

"Many thousand times thousand nights they seek each other, but they meet not. As one single soul they issued forth from the Soul of Souls, the Only One, from the Father and Mother, and drifting lower into the depths they broke into two. Ever since they seek and pursue each other, so as to become one again. And happy is he who finds the half of his soul, for through the union of them all in the mystery of the One the Father and the Mother unite into one, and happiness and mercy radiate onto the earth."

"We have found each other," thought Rachel happily, but she kept silent.

With bated breath the Tzaddik picked up the great folio that was lying in front of him, the *Zohar*, the mysterious Book of Light. A deep fire burned in his eyes as he turned its pages rapidly, and continued:

"Come then, look here, Rachel!"

And Rachel felt as if sparks of blinding hues were flying out of the mysterious pages of the great folio, and miraculous lights were filling the whole room.

"Come, look here, Rachel!"

And the Tzaddik read in the wistful tone of the Book of Lamentations:

"Ever since the Holy of Holies was destroyed, the Hearth

has remained desolate. The Father withdrew, and the Mother wanders forsaken among the ruins. And at this hour, when midnight arrives, the Heavenly Father rises up from His throne, stamps with His feet the heavenly heights so that all the thirteen thousand worlds shake, and He remembers Israel, His Matron, and He cries and cries, and lets two tear drops fall into the great ocean. And at this hour, when midnight comes, the Matron goes up to the ruins of the Holy of Holies, looks at the remains of the Altar, her sacred hearth, and cries and sobs bitterly: 'My couch, my couch, O my sacred resting place, which was covered with a baldachin embellished with precious pearls, where sixty myriad jewels sparkled toward the four winds of the universe, you sustained the world because the Lord of the Universe dwelt in you. Here would come my Lord, take me in His arms, and all my desires would become fulfilled. At this time He would come to me, and rest upon my breast. My couch, my couch, can you remember how we would come to you, full of joy, with enraptured hearts, and thousands of maiden-faced angels with fluttering wings would hurry toward us to receive us with joy? O Holy Ark, you who stood at this spot, from you did light, blessing, and life spread into the world. O tell me, where is my Lord? At this time He would come to me, and I would hear the voice of His approach like unto the tinkling of small silver bells. Now I am here, but He is not, and in the holy place where He would alight now raging dogs bark.' And the Matron sobs and cries, 'O my Lord, my Lord, the light of my eyes has grown dark, O remember how You would embrace and kiss me, Your right arm enveloped me, Your left arm rested under my head, the image of Your countenance shone upon my face like this seal that the king impresses upon his writ, and You vowed that You would never forsake me, saying, If I forget you, let My right hand be forgotten, O Jerusalem!'"

The mysterious words of the Tzaddik shook Rachel to the depth of her being, and she felt that her sorrow was small and insignificant compared to such inexpressibly great anguish. But she sensed that now the great Mysteries, the secrets of the world's sufferings, had opened up to her as well, and that she too could mitigate to a tiny measure the pain of the Matron, that she too could help in building a Temple for the wandering Shekhinah.

"Only a few more nights," she said modestly to the Tzaddik, "and we can begin the building of the Temple."

Full of compassion, the Tzaddik looked at Rachel, at her pale face, sunken cheeks, feverishly burning eyes, and thin, tremulous fingers.

"Mate of my soul, may the Lord of the Universe give you strength!"

And on the thousand and first night, after long and deep reflection, the Tzaddik designated the spot from where all prayers could rise up to Heaven. At the light of torches, singing David's sacred psalms, the believers carried the stones and the implements, and the building of the Temple slowly began. Rachel, feeble and frail, leaned on the arm of the Tzaddik and allowed nobody to approach him lest he be disturbed in his holy meditation. Before a deep trench a big stone cube was supported on two heavy beams: the cornerstone, which the believers knew the Tzaddik would place so that it should be opposite the eternal sacrificial fire of the Heavenly Temple and aligned with the ruined altar of the Holy of Holies of Jerusalem. The Tzaddik, deep in thought, stepped up to the stone, bent

down, and with all his strength tried to push the big stone into the ditch that had been dug for it. But the heavy block did not move. At that moment Rachel knelt down next to him.

"I too want to help in laying the foundation stone of the new Temple."

Rachel strained her weak arms. But suddenly her face was flushed, the veins on her forehead swelled, her body was racked with convulsions, and she fell back unconscious.

"Rachel! Rachel!" cried the Tzaddik, trembling, and horrible fears flooded his heart. "Rachel, did I not say . . . Men! Help!"

The believers came running together in a panic, and their flaming torches threw an eerie light on the deathly pale face of Rachel.

The face of the Tzaddik was distorted by a wild pain. In one moment all the sufferings of the thousand nights' vigils flashed through his heart. He fell broken upon Rachel's body and cried and sobbed aloud.

For several hours the Tzaddik remained prostrate upon the body of Rachel. The believers began to expect that a miracle would take place, that dead Rachel would come back to life.

But when midnight, the hour full of holy lamentations, arrived, the Tzaddik rose, straightened up, and lifting his arms toward Heaven, cried:

"Lord of the Universe! She sat in vigil with me through a thousand nights and shed Your light upon me. If it were in my power, I would raise up my dear spouse and bring her back to life. But I am powerless, a broken vessel. But You, Lord of the Universe, You are omnipotent, why don't You raise up Your dear Matron Israel?"

2

The Old Psalmist

ell, it was enough for today," said David the woodcutter, who was known to everybody by the name "the old psalmist." "It will be enough for a few days," he repeated to himself. "Thank God, it will be enough."

And he leaned his heavy axe against the tree trunk on one of whose stumpy branches hung his small lamp. The forest was cold and foggy, from the breath of the sleeping earth dank mists arose, the birds of the wood were in deep sleep among the branches, and only here and there did a stronger-than-usual blow of old David's axe awaken them. Then a sharp, shrill chirping could be heard in the night, and David, frightened, intoned a Psalm, and quietly crooned the soft melodies of the Hebrew verses, feeling that with his propitiatory words he restored the forest to its nocturnal rest, which he had so sinfully disturbed. The cut branches, the chopped-up pieces of wood, grew into a bigger and bigger pile around him. With trembling hands David tied the fruits of his hard labor into a big bundle and took it upon his bent back to the road where his rickety cart and his tired, winded nag waited impatiently for him. His little lamp now hung from the top button of his coat and threw a sharp light upon the old man's long beard, the white side locks that framed his face, and the deep furrows of his wrinkled cheeks and forehead. If somebody saw from afar the bent, gnomelike, white-headed oldster as he picked his way among the trees while humming his Psalms, he might have thought that a singing dwarf of the forest was moving about in the mysterious night.

The cart slowly filled up. Old David climbed up, sat down on a stump, pulled tight his coat, extinguished his lamp with a strong blow, gee-hoed his ancient horse, and slowly drove off.

By the time he reached the highway dawn was breaking. The stars put on their sparkling white wings and started their own morning Psalms. Tired old David gently urged on his nag, and with only one eye saw the choir of the morning stars. But he quickly rubbed the sleep out of his eyes, and he too intoned a Psalm:

> Praise Him, all ye stars of light.
> Praise Him, O heavens of heavens.

Then Psalm followed Psalm, and though old David had been able to learn only very little in his young years and there was much he did not understand in the text of the sacred songs, the words had become so fused together with his very being that always something of their meaning too lit a spark in his soul.

> Have mercy, O Lord, have mercy
> I am sated with sufferings.

And the hard struggles of long decades streaked across old David's mind. For forty years he had been cutting the trees and lugging them into the little town of Medzibozh. By dawn he had to be in the marketplace, and it was better to arrive early than late, unless he wanted the Baal Shem or the leaseholder Reb Nahum to buy his wood out of pity. As a matter of fact, he did not at all understand why these men paid attention to him, the simple woodcutter, who knew nothing but to murmur a few Psalms. Neither Torah, nor Talmud, nor Kabbalah. But could he be blamed? Had his father been as rich as Reb Nahum, he surely would have sent him to study. As things stood, what else could he do than secretly put from each of his loads of wood a bundle in the courtyard of the Baal Shem? Let those who are fortunate enough to be able to study Torah use it to keep warm . . . Then he entered the synagogue, stopped before the Holy Ark, and sang a few Psalms. This is how he awaited the rise of the sun and the opening of the market. Thereafter he could go home and again start the collecting of wood.

> Much did they torture me since my youth,
> On my back they plowed deep furrows.

But in his youth he had at least had a reason to struggle and suffer. At first for his sick father and mother, then for his wife and child.

> Thy wife is as a fruitful vine in thy house,
> Thy children like olive plants around thy table.

Now he was alone, abandoned, and there was nobody for whose sake he would have to struggle, except himself. He had always eked out a living with the sweat of his brow, and he did not want to eat the bread of charity now in his old age.

When thou eatest the labor of thy hands
Happy shalt thou be and it shall be well with thee.

The Psalms neared their end. By the time David reached the Halleluyah, his cart had come to a rest in front of the little synagogue of Medzibozh. The old psalmist stepped down, washed his hands, and entered the synagogue. The morning rays stole merrily through the windows and the glass of the door, and kissed the silver curtain of the Holy Ark, which began to sparkle so that old David's eyes were almost blinded. He too quickly went up to the Ark, touched the luminous curtain with his lips, and reverently intoned yet another Psalm.

There was as yet nobody else in the synagogue. But in front of it the hurried steps of the awakening town could already be heard. And those who passed in front of the synagogue, and heard the sweetly weeping melody of the matutinal Psalms, knew that the old woodcutter David was pouring out his poor soul before the almighty Lord of the Universe.

When the old psalmist came out of the little synagogue, he experienced a great shock. His cart was not in its place. His aged nag, usually waiting for him with such pious inviting eyes, could be seen nowhere. The blood froze in old David's veins. He took a few tottering steps to the street corner, and strained his eyes searching the distance. His cart had disappeared. Disappeared, together with the gentle animal, and the heavy load of wood, the fruit of so much hard labor. What could have happened? Did the horse go off on its own, or did a ruthless thief drive off with it? Who knows? For a while old David walked up and down the street, inquired from passersby, searched, looked all about, and when he saw that his search was in vain, he accepted the blow of fate with his usual dull resignation to the inevitable. After all, he had lost more, much more, in the course of the long days of his life. And right away he found the Psalm suited for the occasion, and went back into the synagogue, silently murmuring the holy words:

> Some trust in chariots and some in horses,
> But we put our trust in the name of the Lord.

In the meantime a group of people gathered in front of the little synagogue to attend the morning prayer and discussed with compassion the sad loss sustained by the old psalmist.

"Anyway, it was time for the old man to retire."

"But how will he make a living?"

"The congregation will take care of him."

"But he does not want charity."

"He will get some light work in the town."

"Look, Reb Nahum the leaseholder is coming. He can easily give bread to one more person."

"Reb Nahum is now busy with the new Torah scroll."

"This too is Torah. The most important Torah!"

"According to the Baal Shem the simple, faulty Psalm

recitals of the old woodcutter are of greater value than the sparkling Torah study of some *gaon*."

"They surely will not let him starve."

"It seems the oldster is not too downcast. He continues to sing his Psalms with his usual mistakes."

"Hush! The Baal Shem said one must not make fun of the old man, even if he makes mistakes in his recital of the Psalms, for King David in the Other World has never enjoyed the Psalm singing of the earthlings as much as when he listens to the old woodcutter's songs."

"Perhaps the soul of King David lives in the old wood-cutter David."

"He could be one of the thirty-six pious men who maintain the world and can converse with the spirits of the Fathers."

Reb Nahum joined the group, and heard of the mishap that had befallen the old psalmist. When he entered the synagogue he approached old David and said to him:

"From now on you can cut wood in my courtyard, as before, and can help here and there about the house. For that you will get food, and a suit of clothes for Passover and another one for Sukkot."

Old David was happy. But he did not thank Reb Nahum for his goodness. After all, he would still be supporting himself with the work of his hands. He was beholden only to the Lord of the Universe, who had never wholly abandoned him, and to whom King David had once upon a time sung all those holy Psalms.

For weeks there had been much coming and going in the house of Reb Nahum. A great festivity was in the making for the dedication of a new Torah scroll, prepared by the richest Jew of Medzibozh with so much pomp and circumstance that the whole world was abuzz with its wonders. There are those who purchase a Torah scroll all written and ready, and donate it to the synagogue. And there are those who buy the parchment and let a scribe do the writing. For Reb Nahum all this was not enough. He purchased pregnant cows of perfect body, and when they calved he made sure that each time before the calves took a suck some of the mother animals' milk was first taken and given to poor children. Then the calves were fattened on chopfeed, carrots, bran, and other fodder of which a double tithe was given to the poor Kohanites. The most pious ritual slaughterer was brought to kill the fatted calves, and all their meat was distributed among the poor of the town—never before had the poor of Medzibozh enjoyed as much meat as on that occasion. Reb Nahum had the skin of the animals worked up into the finest parchment in his own house by young Jewish tanners who had never before handled the skins of unclean animals. Then he fetched from Lublin the most famous Torah scribe, who sat for months in Reb Nahum's house and penned the sacred letters on the parchment. Each time he reached the name of God, he submerged in the sacred bath before writing it down. Reb Nahum provided the scribe and his whole family with the best of everything. Those who saw what Reb Nahum did were filled with admiration at his limitless generosity. "He spent a whole fortune on the new Torah," they said everywhere.

Finally the new sacred scroll was ready, and Reb Nahum began the preparations for its dedication. Everyone stood agape when they heard of the planned festivities. The most famous rabbis were invited from near and far, and Reb

Nahum made sure in advance to find out what was the favorite food of each of them. In the house the chimney never ceased smoking for days on end, and old David was busy day in, day out, cutting up the wood to keep the fire going, while he continued to murmur his Psalms:

> I have been young and now I am old
> Yet have I not seen the righteous forsaken.

The dedication ceremonies took place in the courtyard under a huge festive tent. The writing of the last letters of the Torah was auctioned off for the benefit of the dowries of the poor girls in town. Those who offered most obtained the privilege of writing the letters. The last letter was written by the Baal Shem himself, and Reb Nahum's face shone with pleasure and joy when he saw the happy conclusion of his great undertaking. The banquet lasted late into the night, and its main delicacies were not the taste of the many cooked and baked dishes, nor the fine aroma of the intoxicating wines of Tokaj and Carmel, but the new songs which the guests had brought along from Lublin, Belz, Sandec, and many other places, and, above all, the holy and mysterious words they heard from the Baal Shem, the great master of the Secrets of Secrets.

Before dawn, when the weight of slumber pressed upon the eyes of the assembled, and only a few were able to stay awake, the Baal Shem indicated to Reb Nahum that it was time to intone the after-meal benedictions before the dawn broke and the time for the morning prayer arrived. Reb Nahum, who, exhausted by the excitements of the day, was himself barely able to keep his eyes open, called out, half-asleep:

"David! Hey, David! Bring water for washing the hands!"
Nobody answered, and Reb Nahum repeated drowsily:
"Where is the woodcutter? Water!"

Old David came in with shuffling steps.

"Where were you?" asked Reb Nahum impatiently.

"Just here, outside the tent, reciting a few verses of the Psalms," replied the old woodcutter timidly.

"Go to hell with your Psalms!" Reb Nahum snapped at him. "Instead, bring water! Don't you see? The Baal Shem is waiting!"

Upon hearing the rude words, the eyes of the Baal Shem flashed. He glanced lovingly at the poor humiliated woodcutter, then looked angrily at Reb Nahum, who, unable to bear the piercing look of the Tzaddik, lowered his eyes and leaned back in his seat as if in a daze.

And then this miracle came to pass:

Before the house of Reb Nahum a dashing carriage suddenly came to a halt. It was the carriage of the squire, and he sent in his servant to tell Reb Nahum that he wanted to talk to him. Reb Nahum, frightened, hurried out into the street, and greeted the count deferentially. But the count, without even listening to what he said, snarled at him angrily that within three days he wanted him out of his land and his tenancy. Reb Nahum entreated him desperately: "Have mercy, my lord, don't reduce me to beggary, have regard for my wife, my children, I would rather pay you double the rent!" The squire paid no attention to him, and repeated his command. Reb Nahum put one foot on the steps of the carriage, leaned into it and begged that the count give him half a year of delay, or at least until after the harvest. The count motioned to the coachman, the coachman gave a pull to the reins, the horses broke into a gallop, and Reb Nahum was dragged along a long way, until finally, in the midst of the forest, he lost his hold, fell down, and fainted. When he came to, he found himself in a strange, dense forest. In the dark of the night he could see nothing, no road, not even a path, only the tall black trees. Shivering, and with dread in his heart, he set out to find his way home. He walked, walked, and it seemed to him as if he were wandering for years in that realm of eternal darkness. He barely remembered what had happened to him. Then a Psalm came to his mind, and he began to recite silently its words:

I will say of the Lord who is my refuge and my fortress,
Thou shalt not be afraid of the terror by night.

Suddenly he saw a shimmering glow in the distance. He set out toward it. A splendid palace appeared, bathed in a blinding light. Blazing rays shone from all the windows as if they were wondrous square moons hovering in the midst of a starry Milky Way. It must be a miraculous palace, thought Reb Nahum. The door was open, and Reb Nahum timidly entered the great hall and, trembling, hid behind the big white stove covered with frost flowers. He was blinded by the dazzling light and was barely able to look around. The walls were crystal fields of frozen light and yet miraculously transparent, so that through them one could see the shining stars of the black firmament, whose cold rays were reflected all about in a thousand colors. Huge dense clusters of diamonds hung down from the ceiling and spread a blinding light in the hall, which was filled with wondrous magical scents. In the middle of the hall was a long green emerald table, and around it in

crystal armchairs sat ancient ones with almost transparent bodies, who seemed to be none other than the patriarchs Abraham, Isaac, Jacob, Moses, Aaron, and David, surrounded by other white-robed figures. They exchanged peculiar, mystical signs, and then one of them, who sat at the head of the table, said:

"Are all the thirty-six here?"

"They are here," answered a deep voice.

"Let us then hear the complaint of King David!"

Reb Nahum shook. An ancient one rose from the table. His head was adorned by a sparkling gold crown, and in his hand he held an eight-stringed lyre, which twanged softly even though no hand touched its strings. And as Reb Nahum looked fearfully into the face of the old king it seemed to him as if the old woodcutter were standing there, straightened up, dignified, crowned, in a white royal robe.

"I have a complaint against the man who stands there in the corner next to the oven."

Reb Nahum shuddered. King David continued:

"He reviled my Psalms into which I poured my heart before the Lord and which give solace and comfort to so many mortals down there on earth."

"He must atone with eternal poverty," a severe voice said. "As a Psalm-singing beggar he will have to wander on endless roads."

Reb Nahum collapsed and heard only through a mist, half-conscious, the well-known voice of the Baal Shem. He begged the old king with moving, compassionate words to forgive the feeble mortal, who today shines in splendor, and tomorrow shivers in the shadow, to allow him to continue in his dust-and-ashes glory, for if he should be allowed to return to his home all haughtiness would leave his heart and in his humbleness he would find solace in King David's beautiful Psalms.

"I forgive him," said the old king. "I forgive him for the sake of the Baal Shem."

At these words Reb Nahum came to, sat up, and looked about him. But he saw neither palace nor forest, only the tent, and there before him stood the old psalmist, the woodcutter David, with the washbasin and the ewer in his hands. And the Baal Shem was still looking at him with a severe reproachful look.

Reb Nahum looked about him astonished. What a peculiar dream he had had in the course of a few moments. Or was it perhaps a vision, a miracle wrought by the Baal Shem or by the old woodcutter? He stood up, gently approached the old psalmist, took the washbasin from his hand and put it down on a stool next to the Baal Shem, and then, gently patting the old woodcutter on the back, he said to him:

"Go ahead and sing your Psalms for a hundred and twenty years. You can always sing them in my house. And I too shall sing with you."

The old woodcutter thanked his master with humble gratitude. And the Baal Shem saw all this, and smiled.

3

Queen Sabbath

e must hurry," Luria said, turning back to his disciples. "The sun is setting and the Queen is approaching."

With quick steps they left the vineyards behind and moved up the slopes of Mount Safed. The slender figure of the young master, a full head taller than all his companions, was wrapped in a white satin robe reaching down to his ankles. The disciples too were clad in festive clothes, and their white headcloths fluttered in the mild evening wind. For a while they kept silent as they walked side by side, lest an inadvertent word disturb the reverential mood of the master.

But soon the excitement overpowered the disciples, and, almost simultaneously, they intoned the Song of Songs, and walked on singing with growing enthusiasm:

Hark! My beloved! Behold he cometh,
Leaping upon the mountains, skipping upon the hills.

Already the faraway mountains were printed purple by the messengers of the approaching Queen Sabbath, who spread violet-colored carpets before the feet of the eagerly expected royal Bride. The song of the disciples grew louder:

O my dove in the clefts of the rock, in the covert of the cliff,
Let me see thy countenance, let me hear thy voice,
For sweet is thy voice and thy countenance is comely.

The swelling tones of the song enraptured the master, and he too began to sing softly:

> Come with me from Lebanon, my bride,
> With me from Lebanon,
> Look from the top of Amana,
> From the top of Senir and Hermon,
> From the lions' dens,
> From the mountains of the leopards.

The air began to cool, the breezes of dusk caressed the fronds of the date-palms and swept a sweet scent into the flushed faces of the master and the disciples. Luria sang almost inaudibly, as if the Song of Songs and the balsamic scents had dazed him:

> Until the day breathe, and the shadows flee away,
> Turn, my beloved, like a gazelle
> Upon the mountains of spices.

They were out of breath when they reached the top of Mount Safed. A wonderful scene spread before their burning eyes. To the east they could see the valley of Gennesaret

and the Jordan. Rows of pomegranate, fig, date, and syca-
more trees divided the valley into narrow strips, and in its
middle hurried the waves of the Jordan, which was lost to
the south in the smooth waters of Lake Gennesaret, surrounded by a crown of dark trees. The purple of dusk
painted a red color over the mirrorlike surface of the lake,
and a red glow enveloped also the olive and palm trees
that framed its banks and lifted their heads proudly toward the flaming sky, as if they too were offering silent
hymns while waiting with outstretched arms for the appearance of the glorious Queen Sabbath. Luria and his
disciples gazed enchanted into the distance, and whispered
the verses of the Song of Songs:

Thou hast ravished my heart, my sister, my bride,
Thou hast ravished my heart with one of thine eyes,
With one bead of thy necklace.

But the master raised his hand, and the disciples fell
silent. Luria's ecstatic soul was aflame with the beauty of
the Sabbath, and dazzling visions opened up before his
eyes.

For a few moments he remained standing motionless
and then spoke with a trembling voice:

"My brothers, I see the Time of Mercy approaching.
Perhaps this is the Sabbath of Sabbaths."

The disciples trembled in rapturous anticipation, but
none of them dared to ask a question. Wordless, they riv-
eted their eyes on the master, as if expecting a miraculous
revelation. Only after a few minutes passed in silence did
Luria's favorite disciple, Hayyim Vital, break the hallowed
silence:

"O Master, reveal to us too the secret of the Sabbath of Sabbaths!"

Luria, as if he had not even heard the words, clasped his hands over his breast, and looked around into the distance. His glance fell on Mount Meron where in the gathering dusk the torches of Ben Yohai's tomb could be seen, and around them the believers, clad in festive white garb, rhythmically swayed in prayer, as if white ghosts of the dead were hovering about the holy tombs.

Luria suddenly turned to his disciples. "If you don't feel it," he said with sadness in his voice, "if you don't see it with your own eyes, don't hear it with your ears, I would tell it to you in vain."

"But, O Master, open our ears! Remove the scales from our eyes, O light of Israel!"

"Do you not see that the air of heaven, near and far, is full of flames, of wandering fires, of souls seeking recovery, redemption?"

"I see it, O Master," whispered Vital, the head of the disciples, with bated breath.

"You can see it, my son, because your soul is a spark from the heights of the Creator's throne, because no dross of earthly sin has become attached to your soul, and its vision has not been dimmed by the stain of primeval sins. But he whose soul is heavy with old and new sins, cannot rise up into the heights, cannot endure the eternal light. He falls back to earth, tired and worn out, into the mire and sludge."

And Luria raised his arms feverishly, and continued:

"The souls wandering about despondently in the oceans of the world are like small ships lost in the dark night of endless seas, always on the lookout and yearning for the appearance of a lighthouse on the horizon, so that they may hurry toward it. Without it they cannot find the way back to their ancestral home, from which they had set out, that home of eternal radiance and pure Light. They wander and err, and ever new waves beat against them and cover them with mud and slime, and the poor, tortured souls cry and whine, and seek refuge . . . until, finally, in the distance, they espy a pure, lofty soul, the beacon, and they swarm toward it, grateful and happy to have found the eternal way."

A flock of ravens circled over the head of the master, with slow, silent beating of wings. Luria looked up at them, and said:

"Perhaps these too are erring souls. And do you see there, on the neighboring hill, the little deer running toward us? Perhaps he too is a seeking, wandering soul. And down there in the valley flow the waters of the Jordan; perhaps its waves too carry fugitive souls toward the holy city, so that they may be able to bathe and become purified, and soar up into the highest Heights, for which they pine and yearn. Do you not hear the song of the souls in the rush of the waters, in the whisper of the boughs, the chirping of birds, the hum of the air, the flight of the clouds and their lightnings? It is the aching song of wounded, suffering souls, which would like to fly home, up into the Hall of Souls, to merge with the Highest Soul from which they were torn away. And the redemption of the world will be complete only when all the erring souls shall be cleansed and return to the Highest, the fragmented sparks become united again, and the soul of the world is filled with the repose of the Sabbath, with peace and mercy."

"And will that be the Sabbath of Sabbaths?" asked Vital impatiently.

"Amid the worries of the weekdays," Luria continued, "the sparks produced by good deeds disintegrate, or hide within opaque, heavy husks. And when the time of the flaming of the souls comes, the sacred moment of receiving Queen Sabbath, the divine Shekhinah, the soul bathes in the lake of purification, and the hidden sparks divest their husks, and flash, hover, naked over the heads. This is the light of Sabbath, the Sabbath soul. And happy is he above whose head a whole wreath of collected sparks hovers and shines, like a sparkling heavenly diadem. It is of these that Scripture says, 'And they that are wise shall shine as the brightness of the firmament. . . .' And the wandering souls, the poor little erring lights, are attracted to the place where the great light shines, where the flame soars up into the heights, and sweeps up and carries with it the little lights, up into the Infinite."

Intoxicated with his own words, Luria embraced Vital, and then, placing his arm on the shoulders of the faithful disciple, advanced a few more steps:

"Come, my friend, to meet the Bride, let us receive the Sabbath."

Alkabez, the young poet, recognized the words of his Sabbath song, and following in the footsteps of the master, continued happily:

> Arise, arise, your light has come,
> Arise, and shed your light,
> Arise and sing a song,
> God's glory is revealed.

The disciples encircled the poet, and sang the refrain in unison:

> Come, my friend, to meet the Bride,
> Let us receive the Sabbath.

The melody of the Sabbath song filled the air, and the surrounding hills echoed faintly the shreds of the joyful words.

"It is the time of Mercy," said Luria in a trembling voice. "Najara, my son, let us hear your Sabbath song too. When you sing, the gates of heaven open, and the angels come down from on high to enjoy it."

Obediently, and with a disciple's humility, Najara intoned his Sabbath song, and the companions hummed it together with him. Luria listened to it silently, dreamily. They reached the last stanza:

> Return to Your Holy of Holies,
> The place where spirits and souls rejoice,
> And sing exalted songs of thanks
> In Jerusalem, the city of beauty.

In the distance, over the crags of Gilead and the summit of Mount Tabor, it seemed as if red lightnings were streaking, as if bloody swords and spears were flashing in the air. From the mountains of Bashan and from the Lebanon red clouds, like hosts of racing horsemen mounted on fiery steeds, rushed in the flames of the dusk toward the Dead Sea and the Eternal City.

Luria suddenly drew himself up to his full length, and turned to his disciples with eyes aflame:

"Do you want to come with me to Jerusalem?"

"To Jerusalem!" exulted Vital. "Let us go. The Time of Mercy is at hand!"

"To Jerusalem!" Luria repeated with passion. "I can see on the distant peaks the crowned Queen, and with her the eternal glory of God. They are going to Jerusalem, and the Palace is being rebuilt, the Throne restored, and the ancient glory shines again. Behold, the Time of Mercy! The heavens open up, all the souls are elevated, and the wandering earthly beings see a great light, soar toward it, and say, 'Up! Let us go in the light of the Lord!' The summit of Lebanon catches fire, the captive of Jerusalem rises from the dust, the daughter of Zion throws off her shackles, and puts on her festive clothes. And she lifts up her eyes and sees, behold, her children all gather from the four winds and flock about her, and her eyes shine and her soul jubilates, saying, 'Who are these who fly like clouds, and like doves toward their nests?' The Sabbath of Sabbaths awaits us in Jerusalem. Come, let us go!"

"To Jerusalem!" the disciples echoed enthusiastically, and they set out after the Master in the gathering mysterious darkness. Luria stopped for a moment and looked around.

"Are all of you here, my children? And what is the matter with you, my son Uzziya, why do your knees tremble?"

The disciple answered modestly and sadly:

"O Master, allow me first to go home and take leave from my loving young bride with whom I celebrated our wedding only this Sukkot and who would despair at my absence. For the road is very long, and the night full of dangers."

"Long and dangerous?" asked Luria, surprised. "If we

want it, we shall be there in a moment, and if the Lord is with us, whom have we to fear?"

"But from Safed to Jerusalem, O Master, the distance is three days' walk, and the dense gloom of dusk has already covered the hills."

Luria gave a start.

For a moment he looked around hesitating, disturbed, with pain in his eyes, as if he had awakened from a deep dream. He felt that all his wonderful visions had all of a sudden disintegrated from the sober words. Everything was over. In place of the dazzling images, high black mountains stood in the darkness. And Luria buried his face into his hands and began to cry aloud.

"Let us go, my holy Master!" begged Vital. "Sadness drives off the light of the Shekhinah, and the Sabbath of Sabbaths is awaiting us in Jerusalem!"

Luria wiped his eyes, looked lovingly at his disciple, and answered despondently:

"It is over, my son. Faintheartedness kills the miracle. Had we all wanted and believed it, it would have come to pass. But one unbeliever can play sad havoc with a thousand believers, and hold back the redemption of the world. The sacred Bride, the Queen of Queens, was waiting for us, but he pined after his young spouse. Come, my sons, let us finish our Friday night prayers and return to the city, to Safed."

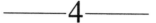

4

The Mystery
of the Bird's Nest

n the darkness of the big courtyard people swarmed like undulating shadows. Jostling, straining, swaying on tiptoe they waited for news from the closely curtained sickroom. Everything had been tried. Messengers were sent on the fastest horses to the nearby saintly men that they should open the Gates of Mercy. For "the captive cannot liberate himself from the house of captivity," and the Tzaddik and his wife are one. Men, the most pious and oldest, gathered frightened in the House of Study, and with their Psalms stormed Heaven for help, all day and all night. A thousand times they wove into the initial letters of holy prayers the name of the Tzaddik's wife, who was suffering in labor. But to no avail. Pale, fasting old women ran into the prayer houses, tore open the doors of the Holy Ark, and cried desperate supplications at the shaking holy scrolls. Even the cemetery was measured, forgiveness was whispered into the graves, and the dead were petitioned. The ten men assembled and, invoking the higher power, changed the name of the suffering woman, so that the cruel emissary of Fate should not be able to find her. But perhaps he wanted to smite the expected child, whose future name, that of a boy or of a girl, only the heavenly Seraphim and Cherubim could know.

And when nothing helped, they sent for the professor whose name and fame were praised in many lands. What a humiliation. To expect from the intervention of human hands what they were unable to obtain by imploring the infinite Heavens, the highest powers!

"Quiet! Quiet!" the people whispered to each other in the dark courtyard. "We could be heard inside!"

From time to time the door of the great House of Study opened, and the light that poured out through it illuminated the worrisome faces of those standing in the courtyard. An old man from among those who sat poring over the holy books came out and asked: "Has help come yet?" And then, sighing, went back and closed the door behind him.

Midnight arrived. From the House of Study faint snatches of the midnight laments could be heard:

> A voice is heard in Ramah,
> Lamentation, bitter weeping,
> Rachel weeping for her children.

And then a sharp voice interrupted, shrieking the sequel:

> Thus saith the Lord:
> Refrain thy voice from weeping,
> And thine eyes from tears.

For there is hope for thy future,
And thy children shall return to their border.

Suddenly the clatter of wheels interrupted the silence of the night. A carriage stopped in front of the open gate. By the dim light of the lamps they could see a man, clad in black, jump down, with a little satchel in his hand. He was followed by a white-clad woman carrying a package.

"The professor! The professor has arrived!" they whispered in the courtyard. Quickly, with awed respect, they opened a path for him to cross the courtyard. At a few steps' height over the courtyard the door to the Room of Books opened. One could see the professor meet the Tzaddik, exchange a few words with him, and instantly enter the sickroom. The odor of carbol wafted out through the openings of the windows. Then the bubbling of a small kettle could be heard. The surgery instruments were being boiled, cleansed. Silhouettes of ghostly figures could be seen moving across the curtains. The assistant helped the professor to dress. She held up for him a long white gown, tied it with white strings around his neck and wrists. Now, she moved as if to crown him with a tall, white bonnet. And as he stepped up to the hot cauldron, and lifted up its lid, dense steam rose before his face, and he seemed like a mystical priest swinging an incense-burner before the altar of a temple. Quickly he replaced the lid, looked up at the clock on the wall, and then walked over into the Room of Books.

There they stood, opposite one another, the great professor in his white gown and the great Tzaddik in his white caftan, like two representatives of the earthly and heavenly powers brought face-to-face by incomprehensible forces.

"While my instruments boil," said the professor, smiling, "we can chat for a few minutes. Do not worry. There will be no problem."

"With the help of the Almighty," added the Tzaddik. "Everything depends on Him."

"And a little bit on the success of my hands," said the professor jocularly.

"The success of your hands too is in the hands of the Almighty."

"A surgical operation and theological disputation do not harmonize," said the professor, cutting short any further argument. His glance fell on the big folio that stood open on the rabbi's reading desk, ready to be delved into. He asked jovially:

"What are you investigating at this late hour, Rabbi?"

"It is the *Zohar*, the Book of Splendor," answered the Tzaddik. "The collection of mysteries."

"Mysteries?" marveled the professor. "Some kind of superstitious beliefs? Conjuration of spirits?"

"No!" responded the Tzaddik seriously. "It is written, 'There is no enchantment with Jacob, neither is there any divination with Israel.' These are deep, mysterious teachings. It is difficult to explain."

"Still, Rabbi, perhaps I would be able to understand something of it."

The Tzaddik hesitated. Should he reveal the pearls to the unqualified? Who, for all he knew, would hold them up to ridicule? But when he looked into the eyes of the professor, he saw in them the pure fire of craving for knowledge, and the thought crossed his mind that perhaps it would be a sanctification of the Name of the Lord to let something of the Book of Splendor radiate into the soul of this stranger.

"This passage here in the chapter of Creation speaks of husband, wife, and the child to be born. It is difficult to translate it into another language, but I shall try.

"About the creation of Adam and Eve it is written, 'and God blessed *them*,' and it is also written, 'in the image of God created He *him*.' Is there no contradiction here? We must understand that the Creator of the Universe called both of them, man and woman together, by the name Adam, man. They are like the flame that hovers on the wick, and does not separate from it, and their ascent is possible only together.

"Come and see the depths of Scripture. A bird flies up every night into the Garden of Eden, its wings are blazing flames, its beak is glowing fire, and it alights on the boughs of the Tree of Life, and looks into the Hall of the Souls. This is the hidden meaning of what the Book of Creation says, 'there went up a mist from the earth . . . and a river went out of Eden. . . .' This is the woman's yearning for the man, when the Upper Waters unite with the Lower Waters, and fertility floods the world. But when the blessing is lost in sterility, that is what the lament of the prophet bemoans, 'And the water shall fail from the sea, and the river shall be drained dry.' Then the Tree of Life becomes weak, and the Tree of Death gains power. Yet the Song of Songs sings of the fruitful kisses, 'Let him kiss me with the kisses of his mouth.' As it is written, 'And Jacob kissed Rachel.' Soul cleaves to soul, and on High, in the Hall of Souls, in the Bird's Nest, a new light is ignited, and it shines and increases the glorious light of the Heavenly Throne. . . . This is the mystery of the verse, 'Blessings of heaven above, blessings of the deep that couches beneath, blessings of the breasts and of the wombs . . . unto the utmost bounds of the everlasting hills.'"

"And do the simple human desires," interrupted him the professor, "which God implanted into man, have no place and rights of their own?"

"Why would He have implanted desires into him without a purpose?" asked the Tzaddik gently. "Why should He have placed His crown upon the head of man, and why should He have shaped man in His image, if thereafter man could have no share in the formation of the Upper Worlds? Behold, here we read, 'Ever since the primeval days yearning souls tarry in the Hall of Souls, hidden in the light that shines from one end of the world to the other, and wait to find their redemption in the union of man and woman. Of this speaks the Psalm, 'For the leader, upon the maidens.' But there are maidens who do not sing; whom no song of the cradle, no chirping of the bird's nest, awaits. Letters burn and flame from beneath but cannot unite with the letters of the Above. About this the Book of Creation says, 'Is man a tree of the field?' A dry cinder, grown cold, which has no flame, no light, and the soul suffers in the dark and increases the power of darkness . . ."

"These are beautiful symbols," the professor interrupted him, "and beautiful teachings! The modern state too is engaged in a fight against sterility, for the future of the nation. But does one not have to take into account the nature of frail man, and the woman's fear?"

"And why do they not fear the Almighty, who can take back His gift, life, at any moment?" asked the Tzaddik gently. "See, here we read, 'Redemption of the world of

the Lord cannot come until the Hall of Souls is emptied of all the souls. And he who sins against this, of him Scripture says, 'Whoso robbeth his father or his mother, and saith, It is no transgression, the same is the companion of a destroyer.' What is the meaning of this? Come, see the mystery of the words: his father is the heavenly Father, blessed be His name, and his mother is the Community of Israel. And see how wrathful are the words of the prophet, when he condemns 'those who slay the children.'

"On high, in the Hall of Love, among the boughs of the grove of nut trees, in the Bird's Nest, the Holy One seeks out the holy soul, takes it by the hands, kisses it and caresses it, and raises it up to Himself, playing with it as a father plays with his beloved child: 'My dove with the purple wings, my innocent.' Thus He lets it descend and start on its terrestrial way, and He follows it with His eyes, observes it from the Heights, anxiously, protectively. . . ."

The professor listened amazed to the mystical words of the Rabbi and almost envied him for this strong faith. A word hovered on his lips, but at that moment the door leading to the next room opened, and a white-clad figure appeared:

"Doctor, everything is ready."

The professor quickly rose, and followed his assistant. The Tzaddik remained alone and tried to continue reading the Book of Splendor. But the letters fluttered in a haze before his eyes. His thoughts were drawn to the other room in which the intervention of a human hand was deciding between life and death. Why did the Almighty give so much power into the hands of mortal man? Has He no other ways? Or is this too one of His mysteries? Does He wish to make His creature a partner in the secrets of Creation?

He again directed his eyes to the book and tried to read. But he could only stare, stare at the letters. Still, even the mere looking at the Book of Splendor means blessing. But perhaps it would be better now to pray, to recite Psalms, to cry for the saving of a life.

Or perhaps for two lives? And if for one, for which of the two? Behold, here was before him the awesome mystery of the bird's nest, about which the sacred commandment says, "Thou shalt let the mother go, but the young thou mayest take unto thyself." A frightening thought.

Oh, if only the waiting were over!

The Tzaddik rose, and began walking up and down in his room. He recited, one after the other, those Psalms whose initial letters were the same as the letters in the name of the gravely ill woman. And it seemed to him as if he could hear from the House of Prayer the voices of the believers, who were reciting the same Psalms. Perhaps the whole universe was praying with him, and here, in his room, the letters of the holy books flew up and awakened the supernal letters to plead for mercy at the footstool of the Compassionate One.

He stepped before the Holy Ark, which stood in the corner on a small platform, and pressed his forehead against the velvet of the curtain. His temples throbbed as if they were about to burst. A cry broke forth from his lips:

"Do not punish her, my Father. Let me rather be the atoning sacrifice."

And, exhausted, he sank onto the chair next to the Ark.

The door of the sickroom opened. The professor entered, his white gown bespattered with blood: He pushed the protective mask up onto his forehead, and his eyes shone with excitement.

"The patient is saved, Rabbi. She needs complete rest now."

"And the child?" cried the Tzaddik, and his voice trembled.

"I shall explain everything," answered the professor. "Here, sit down for a moment. Afterward we can talk about the mystery of the bird's nest."

When they sat side by side, the professor turned to the Tzaddik, got hold of his hand, and looked at him sorrowfully, as if he wanted to prepare him for a heavy blow. He hesitated for a moment, and then said:

"It was a very difficult case, Rabbi. Moreover, to make sure that the operation succeeded it was necessary, alas, to prevent the possibility of future offspring."

"Woe that the Holy One thus punished the two of us!" cried the Tzaddik, and snatched away his hand from the hand of the professor, as if it were the hand of a murderer.

The tenderness of the Tzaddik to his convalescent wife knew no bounds. Several times a day he interrupted his studies, and paid a visit to the sickroom to comfort and strengthen her with the warmth of his eyes, of his words. Some of the believers even thought that the visits were too much, when the room of the Tzaddik was full of people asking for advice, waiting to be instructed, and hoping for blessings. But is visiting the sick not a sacred commandment? Is it not written that divine Glory hovers over the head of the sick? And that he who visits the sick takes away one-sixtieth of his illness?

But as the recuperation progressed, sadness grew in the

heart of the Tzaddik. The shadow of gloomy days pressed down on his soul.

And when, after full recovery, the people of the house wanted to return the couch of the Tzaddik from the Room of Books to its old place, he stopped them with a sorrowful, listless look, and said sadly:

"Leave it where it is. If the Almighty, blessed be His name, smote us this much, what is the good in dalliance?"

5

The Moon of the Tzaddik of Lublin

he strength of the emaciated body of the Tzaddik of Lublin was gradually ebbing away. And those who had the fate of the Universe at heart began to fear that the pillar of the world would fall, and there would be no one to take his place. The believers took to making the pilgrimage to the old Master more frequently, and were anxiously awaiting the moment when he would declare himself and place his hand upon the head of one of his veteran disciples to consecrate him as his successor. They sat around him in silent humility. Who would be so audacious as to express, even in a vaguest hint, the concern of his soul? Only deep in their hearts did the painful question become more aching, more disquieting, more lacerating: who will fill his place?

"And what objection is there against me?" said suddenly young Reb Hershele of Zadichov, riveting his burning black eyes on the Master, who was reclining on the couch.

"Quiet! Quiet! Who has ever heard such a thing?" were heard round about indignant, scandalized voices. But young Reb Hershele straightened up to the full length of his angular figure, stepped up to the Tzaddik, and addressed him directly:

"Rabbi, why do we make a secret of this? The anxiety about the future burns in the hearts of all of us. In the souls of all of us quivers the question: who will be the successor? And I ask, what objection is there against me?"

"Unheard-of impudence! Who is thinking of you? Nobody!" they cried all around. But Reb Hershele continued undisturbed:

"Rabbi, I ask myself whether I am worthy. Day and night I delve into the secrets and miracles of the Torah. I have consecrated my body to be a pure vessel. There is no moment when my eyes do not search for the mysteries of mysteries. I have sought and found new paths in our sacred teachings. My life flows unblemished in waters as pure as crystal. What objection, then, is there against me?"

"Let others praise you, not your own mouth!" quoted the men all about. "Who has ever heard such a thing? Who was thinking of him?"

The Tzaddik of Lublin raised his head, fixed a long, penetrating glance at the young man who stood before him, and said gently:

"You are right, my son, you are right, Reb Hershele."

Then he turned to the grumbling believers:

"Calm yourselves, my children. The innocence with which Reb Hershele can enumerate, without any bashfulness, the proofs of his greatness is in itself the highest degree of modesty."

Outside the day was fading. The setting sun sent red streaks of light through the window.

"Take the lead in the *Minhah* prayer, Reb Hershele!" said the Tzaddik.

The youth of Zadichov obediently stepped up to the reading desk. The disciples recited the Eighteen Benedictions silently, with closed eyes, swaying rhythmically. One or the other of them opened his eyes for a moment and saw with astonishment that the youth of Zadichov was standing motionless in his place, and a wreath of flames was shining over his head.

After the *Minhah* all of them looked upon Reb Hershele as upon the heir of Splendor.

But Reb Hershele continued to make the pilgrimage to his Master in Lublin on every holiday. He sent to the Lubliner also the believers who turned to him. In vain did the Tzaddik of Lublin say to them, "You do not have to come here any longer. The light already shines there in Zadichov." Reb Hershele and his followers missed no opportunity to kindle the festive fire of their souls at the flickering torch of Lublin. The more so, since the illness of the Tzaddik of Lublin made it a sacred duty to visit him frequently. "He who visits the sick takes away one-sixtieth of his illness." And Reb Hershele would have been glad to take upon himself all the sufferings of his Master.

It was the evening of the outgoing Day of Atonement. The Tzaddik had triumphantly vanquished the long fast. He was lying on his couch, and listening with pleasure to the sweet melody of the *Neilah* prayer sung by Reb Hershele. It was like the music of the spheres for him. He saw, he heard, that On High, before the Heavenly Throne, they said approvingly, "The Lubliner did well in choosing a replacement. Now he can come up." How beautiful it would be to rise up thus, in whiteness, in the glow of the heavenly atonement, into the World of Eternity and of Eternal Truth!

The Tzaddik looked out the window. The firmament was covered with dense clouds. Not a single star could be seen. The Moon, too, was probably hidden, even though on this night, after the Day of Atonement, it was his custom to sanctify the New Moon. The Moon, which was the symbol of Israel, which wanders palely around the earth at nighttime and eternally waits for its light from the Sun.

He wanted to rise and go to the door, to look out on the other side, where the Moon would be at this time, to see whether the sky was clear. He leaned against the armrest and tried to rise. But he fell back feebly. The believers hurried over to arrange his pillows.

"It is nothing, nothing," the Tzaddik reassured them. "Blow the *shofar!*"

The long blast filled the prayer room of the Tzaddik: the great *Tekiah*, which announces from one end of the world to the other that the Sentence has been sealed, and the Book of Judgment closed. They hurriedly recited the evening prayer. Blessing Him who "with His word brings about the evenings, with wisdom opens the gates, with understanding changes the times, and arranges the stars on their watches according to His will in the firmament of Heaven, creates day and night, rolls up light before darkness, and darkness before light. . . ."

When the prayer was finished, Reb Hershele stepped up to the Tzaddik, took his hand gently, and asked in a low voice:

"How does the Master feel?"

The Lubliner answered painfully:

"I need the Moon, Reb Hershele. Perhaps I can still, for a last time, sanctify and bless her. Now, in the hour of purification and grace. . . ."

"The whole firmament is covered with dark clouds," interjected one of the believers.

A deep, sobbing sigh broke forth from the Tzaddik's chest. The eyes of Reb Hershele filled with compassion. With caressing love he looked at the old man. Then suddenly he bent down to him, gently raised the head of the Tzaddik, and supporting it with his arm turned it toward the window:

"Look there, Rabbi, there is the Moon, waiting."

The Tzaddik raised his heavy eyelids, and his face lighted up. For a long while his eyes remained fixed on the open window. Then he began to whisper the prayer of the Moon's Consecration. "Halleluyah! Praise the Lord in heavens, praise Him in the Heights! Praise Him, all ye His angels, praise Him all His hosts! Praise Him, O Sun and Moon, praise Him all the stars of light."

The believers silently prayed with him: "And He spoke to the Moon that she should be renewed, a wreath of glory for those that are carried from the womb, and who will be renewed like her."

The Tzaddik raised his head somewhat, to continue with the passage, in reciting which he was wont to dance a few steps in the light of the Moon: "As I dance toward you, and cannot reach you, so my enemies should not be able to reach and harm me." But suddenly his head fell back onto the arm of Reb Hershele.

"Is the Moon still there, my son Reb Hershele? It seems to me that she disappeared."

"There she shines, Rabbi. Continue the prayer," answered Reb Hershele.

The Tzaddik looked up, and, straining his voice, whispered the watchwords that in ancient warlike times the liberators of the Land of Israel breathed into each other's ears at their secret meetings held under the light of the Moon: "David, king of Israel, lives! David, king of Israel, lives! David, king of Israel, lives!"

The believers repeated after him three times, in a loud voice: "David, king of Israel, lives!"

"Peace be upon you!" the Tzaddik continued, turning to Reb Hershele.

"Upon you be peace!" answered Reb Hershele humbly.

"Peace be upon you! Peace be upon you!" He turned to the believers, right and left.

"Upon you be peace!" they all replied together, in a sad, low voice, as if they were bidding farewell.

"I think, my children, that you do not see the Moon," said the Tzaddik, troubled again. "You are not reciting the benediction with true zeal. But the Moon needs our blessing, so that she can receive the light of her bridegroom, the Sun, properly adorned. Perhaps you don't even see the Moon."

"There she shines, over the window," said Reb Hershele, and continued the prayer so that the thoughts of the Master should not go astray: "Hark! My beloved! behold, he cometh, leaping upon the mountains, skipping upon the hills. My beloved is like a gazelle or a young hart. Behold, he standeth behind our wall, he looketh through the windows, he peereth through the lattice."

The Tzaddik, looking at the window, continued with his voice raised:

"Who is this that cometh up from the wilderness, leaning upon her beloved? May it be Your will, O our God, to repair the waning of the Moon, and let the light of the Moon be like the light of the Sun, as it was in the seven days of Creation, before she was reduced, as it is written, 'the two great luminaries.' And let the word of Scripture be fulfilled, 'and they will seek the Lord and David their king.' Amen."

Reb Hershele let the head of the Tzaddik lean back against the heaped-up pillows. The Tzaddik rested for a few moments with closed eyes and then raised the heavy curtain of his eyelids and looked around. He placed his right hand upon the head of Reb Hershele, and spoke with happiness in his voice:

"Be blessed, Reb Hershele, be blessed. And bless me, Reb Hershele, before my great journey. Happy is your lot, Reb Hershele. I had known well that you could perform great things, that the clouds readily obey your command and dissolve from before the face of the Moon. But that the order of Creation is changed at your word, the placement and the course of the stars of the firmament, that at your command they trouble the Moon to come before my window where she had never before shed her light, this I would not have thought had my own eyes not seen it. Happy is your lot, Reb Hershele, my shining, pure Moon."

The believers listened with awe and compassion to the fading voice of the Tzaddik, and all of them knew that what the Lubliner saw with his eyes looking into the distance was the purest truth and reality, even if their own weak eyes could perceive nothing of it.

But in the holy moment, when the Tzaddik of Lublin gave back his soul to the Lord of the Universe, everyone saw that the room filled with a miraculous light, as if moonlight had framed the couch on which the Tzaddik lay with a pale, shining countenance. Or was it the shining farewell kiss of the Shekhinah?

—6—

Struggle with the Evil One

awn had barely broken when little Avromele suddenly awakened, stretched his limbs, then rubbed his eyes and looked around sleepily. At the head of his bed on the naked floor stood a big white washbasin, and next to it a big two-eared mug full of water. Avromele shook, as if the cold water had run down his warm body. For a moment he hid under his feather bed, and closed his eyes. But then he saw before him his master, standing up in class and reading from the big book of *The Way of Life*: "Be strong like a lion to get up in the morning in the service of your Creator, to be the awakener of dawn." And he imagined that his classmates already sat around the big table and studied, and he was the one to arrive shamefacedly in the last moment. "Just one more minute," he thought, "and I too shall be strong as a lion." But he began to have compunctions. He had been awake for quite a while, and had not yet recited the morning prayer. And he remembered the words of his mother, that immediately upon awakening he should rinse his hands, and especially the fingers around the nails, lest an evil spirit worm itself into them and possess him. If a child, before going to bed, recited his prayers piously, all night good angels watched over him, on his right Michael, on his left Gabriel, before him Uriel, and over his head the Glory of God. The wandering evil spirits lurked in vain in the dark, they did not dare even as much as approach the bed. But once he woke up, the heavenly hosts flew back up into the Heights, and then he had to be pure, and must tie himself with prayers to the Almighty, so that nobody could harm him.

Avromele wanted to jump out of the bed, but felt as if a strong hand had pushed his head back into the pillow. And strange, tempting thoughts surged through his mind. Perhaps it was not even true what his mother so often had told him. Perhaps evil spirits did not exist, and neither did angels. Perhaps all that was a story, told to children, so that they keep their hands clean and pray every morning. But he was a big boy already, soon he would be thirteen, and would celebrate his *bar mitzvah*. He was strong like a young lion, and was not afraid.

He would try to get up today without washing his hands, and go to school and tell the other boys that all that was a story!

He quickly threw off the feather bed, and sat up.

Suddenly a cold shiver ran over his body. Opposite, the door opened of itself. He saw nobody behind it, nor saw anybody enter. Only as if a light breeze flitted in the semi-darkness, and as it moved toward the bed Avromele broke into a cold sweat. He tried to cry out, but felt that an un-

seen ice-cold hand pressed upon his mouth. Anyway, he
would cry in vain: nobody was at home. His father was on
his way to a fair, and his mother would go at this hour to
the slaughterer with a chicken. At this thought it seemed
to him as if somebody were holding a cold knife against
his throat. He started to scream, but no sound issued from
his throat. He fell back on the bed, and felt that the evil
spirit was entering through his open mouth, taking possession of his heart, his lungs, and his whole being, overpowering every drop of his blood, every sinew of his body,
and he was helplessly delivered into its hands.

He would have liked to remain motionless in his bed, to
wait until his mother returned; perhaps she could help him.
But the spirit, as if it had grabbed him from inside, made
him sit up, straightened his back, and forced him to stand.

"Put on your clothes, and let us go out into the street,"
the spirit commanded him, and Avromele was forced to
obey. Once outside, he walked as if in a state of semicon-
sciousness. People passed him, but he did not recognize
them, did not even know their names, and did not dare to
speak to them. Slowly he approached the synagogue, from
which the chant of loud prayers issued. Avromele was
seized with a powerful desire. He wanted to enter, to pray
for mercy, to ask help. But the evil spirit gave him a powerful tug from the inside, and made him turn away.

"Anywhere but there!" the spirit commanded in a shrill,
frightened voice. "Anywhere but there! I did not take possession of you so that you would lead me into the house
whose name I am not even allowed to pronounce!"

Avromele groaned with pain, and turned back heartsick.
Silently he turned into the street of his school. Through
the windows of the small study room the light of candles

could still be seen. Inside, small boys were sitting bent over big books, and their chanting was perceived by Avromele as the melody of a wonderful, enticing song. He quickly stepped to the window.

"Again you want to take me to a place where they work against me!" cried the evil spirit inside Avromele, shaking his whole body, and with a powerful, cruel push hurled him to the other end of the street.

Avromele fell unconscious into the mud of the street. For a long time he lay there in a faint, and when he came to he felt that he could do nothing more. He must blindly obey the spirit, do what it wanted, and wait until it departed, or until a holy man expelled it by force. He lay where he was and awaited the command of the spirit. But the spirit began to groan and to wail.

"The time of my prayer has arrived! Woe to me, woe to me! How long must I wander accursed in the world!? When does the hour, the hour of my redemption, come?"

And it turned Avromele's hands toward a big rock that was lying there next to him. Avromele took hold of it, easily uprooted it from the earth, then he lay back and raised it high above him, and with all his strength brought it down upon his breast, so that the thud and the resonance of his chest could be heard from afar, like the pounding of a giant hammer upon an anvil. The spirit moaned horribly inside him and recited the words of the confession of sins:

"We have sinned, we have betrayed, we have robbed, we have spoken evil."

Each word was followed by a blow of the huge stone, until Avromele's coat was torn to shreds, and the blood flowed from his chest. People gathered around him, and looked with pity at the agony of the possessed boy.

"We must call the holy rabbi," said a white-bearded old man.

The spirit implored them:

"Oh, woe, do not call him. It is from him that I run, from him that I try to hide."

A few minutes later the Tzaddik arrived. For a while he looked wordlessly at the boy, then, murmuring a silent prayer, he bent down over him. The spirit cried out in pain:

"Do not hurt me, O holy man, I have already suffered enough!"

The Tzaddik addressed him with a stern command:

"Tell me your name, and the name of your mother, who you are, what is your sin, and then leave the body of the boy. Then I shall pray for you, so that you find rest, and the angels of destruction should no longer pursue you and hurt you."

The spirit burst into a satanic laughter:

"What is your power to be able to save me? A thousand times thousand spirits of perdition lie in ambush for me, waiting that I should leave the pure body of the boy which they cannot approach. If I leave this place of refuge they will start pursuing me again, will torture me, put me in a sling and hurl me from one end of the world to the other, and there will come the evil demons whom I myself have created with my sins, and will hit me in the face and whip me, and drive me without surcease. How could you save me from this terrible host?"

"Get hold of him and bring him into the synagogue," the Tzaddik ordered the believers who stood about. But nobody dared to touch the boy.

"Simon and Hayyim, lift him up and bring him into the synagogue," repeated the Tzaddik sternly.

The disciples obeyed without a word, and, trembling, approached Avromele. The boy began to writhe and struggle, threw himself about, whimpered and moaned, and the spirit again spoke out of the tossing and turning body:

"If you force me to leave his body I shall kill him. I shall go out through his throat and choke him."

The Tzaddik snapped at him coldly:

"I command you to exit through the small toe of his left foot, so that he should come to no harm!"

The spirit, as if it coiled itself up in the boy's body, made no move.

"Tie him up, and let us go!" said the Tzaddik.

Simon and Hayyim obeyed. The procession started out, with the Tzaddik in the lead, followed by the two disciples who carried Avromele, and after them a big crowd of people—men, women, and children.

The big dark synagogue, lighted up only by seven long candles, filled in a moment. The seven candles were held by seven old men who, clad in white shrouds, stood before the Holy Ark.

The tied-up body of the boy was placed on the reading platform opposite the Ark. Avromele lowered his eyes—the spirit did not allow him to look at the Holy Ark.

"Open the Ark!" commanded the Tzaddik.

A terrible scream broke out of Avromele's mouth.

"Have mercy! Have compassion!" begged the spirit. "You are compassionate, you pity this innocent boy, who sinned only once, why do you not have pity on me, with the horrible host of my sins of which I repent? Why are you delivering me back into the hands of my torturers?"

"Leave his body in peace," answered the Tzaddik in a soft, touched voice, "and we shall pray for you every day in this holy place, shall distribute alms for your salvation, shall measure the cemetery with candles and light them in the synagogue for your redemption. The Creator will forgive your sins, and will give you rest under the wings of His protection. Leave in peace."

"Let me stay at least for twelve more months!" entreated the spirit. "Before that I cannot leave."

"Take out the Torah scrolls and carry them around!" cried the Tzaddik.

White figures, clad in the garb of Yom Kippur and covered with white prayer shawls, hurried to the Holy Ark and took out the sacred scrolls. Accompanied by the old men who carried the long burning candles, they circled the platform on which Avromele writhed in agony. The spirit constantly turned his face away from the Torah scrolls, and the boy was forced to turn around and around on the platform, hiding, moaning, like an enchanted lurching spindle.

Seven times they went around the platform with the sacred scrolls, and the power of the spirit diminished visibly. The boy grew more quiet.

"Give me only twelve more days!" begged the spirit in a crying, humble voice.

The sacred procession stopped.

"Have pity for at least twelve more hours!" implored the spirit.

"Swear by the Almighty God," cried the Tzaddik, "that in twelve hours you will leave the body of the boy and will cause no harm to anybody, neither here in the synagogue nor outside in the street. Swear by the name of the Almighty God!"

"Oh, woe to me!" cried the spirit, "I, Samuel, the sinful son of Rachel, cannot utter that word. Oh, if I could utter

it the evil demons would have no power over me. Pray for
me, and ask for my redemption!"

The spirit began to sob, convulsively, chokingly, writh-
ing and shaking, and the whole synagogue cried with him
in pity.

The Tzaddik bent his head deeply into the Holy Ark,
and silently whispered the ineffable, redeeming sacred
Names. Then, suddenly he straightened up:

"Extinguish the candles, and blow the *shofars!*"

The seven candles went out, and the fearsome sound
of seven *shofars* wailed in the dark synagogue.

Every heart trembled, every soul shook in fear. Now the
spirit had no choice but to leave. Holy God, Lord of the
Universe! Let nothing bad happen!

Suddenly, it was as if a thin faint ray had shot through
the darkness from the platform toward the window. The
glass of the window made a cracking sound and fell down
clanging on the floor of the synagogue.

Little Avromele awoke at the noise of the clatter, and
quickly jumped out of his bed. He clutched his head. Was
it a dream or a mirage, or had a miracle really taken place?
The big white washbasin was still standing next to his bed,
and with it the big two-eared mug full of water. Avromele
quickly grabbed the mug, poured water on his hands,
wiped them on his sheet, and recited devoutly the Prayer
of Awakening, giving thanks to the Eternal King that He
had restored his soul unto him in His boundless mercy.
Then he dressed and hurried to the school, where his classmates received him with a little malicious glee:

"Well, diligent Avromele, this time you too came late."

——7——

The Booth of Rymanow

he Tzaddik of Rymanow never liked the great pomp and circumstance with which they celebrated Sukkot, the Feast of Booths, in Berdichev. He disliked it that they constructed a booth that could have stood for a palace. And that they walked about with the fruit of the Hadar tree, the palm branch, and the myrtle twig as if they were symbols of a triumphant achievement.

"Where is the triumph?" he was wont to ask. "Where is the triumph? After all, the sentence is sealed only on the day of the Hosannas, and who would dare to forestall the divine judgment?"

Otherwise, too, the Rymanower had quite a different view of the Feast of Booths than the Berdichever. The Berdichever in general took the great Holy Days lightly. Never could a tear be seen in his eyes. He walked about jubilantly in his white robe, like somebody who is quite sure of himself. "God must forgive," he would say. And he always knew what he was saying.

"Why does Scripture say, 'Happy is the people that know the joyful blast,' the blast of the *shofar*? The sound of the *shofar* forces God to get down from the Throne of Justice and sit on the Throne of Mercy. And do you know what happens on the Throne of Mercy? First of all, when the good deeds and the sins of man are put on the scales, God adds to the scale of good deeds those good deeds that man in his thoughts *wanted* to do, but in reality did not do. And is there anybody who did not *want* to do more good deeds than the number of bad deeds he actually did commit? And if nevertheless a person is found whose sins outweigh the good deeds, what does the Infinite Mercy, blessed be His name, do? He sends off the heavenly accusers to undertake a search for additional sins, and while the sons of Satan are away God removes the heaviest sins from the scales, and hides them under His throne. And when the demons return with the new aggravating data, they look in vain for the old sins, as it is written, 'In all my labors they shall find in me no iniquity that were sin.'"

But the Rymanower remarked quietly:

"But is it not written, 'Thou shalt not steal'?"

The Berdichever Tzaddik truly considered the Feast of Booths a feast of triumph, and he tried to give it the greatest possible splendor and magnificence. "We must fill our souls," he said, "with joy, so that we should receive the Feast of the Torah with the greatest possible jubilation, and the seven days are barely enough for that."

But according to the Rymanower, the most difficult part of the work had to be performed precisely in these seven days, for until the Day of the Hosannas the sentence was still undecided, so that everything depended precisely on these seven days.

The Tzaddik of Rymanow set up a simple canvas booth. He had the gray walls covered on the inside with white cloth, and on the dense oak branches of the roof he hung a few clusters of grapes and a little vial of oil from the Mount of Olives. This was the only decoration of the booth. One must not shame the poor, he said. These seven days are the feast of equality. The Children of Israel must show that they know no differences among themselves. There is no difference between rich and poor, between palace and hut. For all of us are dwellers of shaky booths.

It happened in the year in which the Tzaddik of Rymanow extended by more than two hours the fast of the Day of Atonement. It was necessary to invalidate grave accusations On High. Almost insurmountable obstacles had to be overcome. When the Tzaddik finally left the synagogue, before eating or drinking anything, he instantly began working on the construction of the booth. At other times it was his wont to hammer only one stake into the earth in order to make a beginning in the sacred work. Now he did not rest until he assembled the whole booth. It was midnight by the time he sat down to his supper.

That this had very great significance was understood by everyone who had eyes to see and ears to hear. Those who were with the Tzaddik in the courtyard watched how, under the moonlight, he hammered in stake after stake, and in the meantime recited in a sorrowful, crying voice, the words of the Psalm:

He concealeth me in His pavilion in the day of evil,
He hideth me in the covert of His tent.

They observed, awestruck, the white-haired Tzaddik standing on the ladder, with his beard getting caught in the branches as he lifted them up to the roof, while from his eyes great teardrops fell on the oak leaves; and those who could see and hear knew in advance that a great event was in the making.

On the eve of Sukkot, when the believers came out of the synagogue, a great storm was brewing. The high wind caught up and twirled around the dust and the dry leaves, and hurled them into their faces. They were able to proceed only by protecting their eyes with their coatsleeves. Some of them began to consider whether in such an infernal storm it was at all necessary to make use of the booth. Others were worried lest the wind topple the booth, and the festive candles cause everything to catch fire.

But the Tzaddik struggled on toward his house, without a word, and directly entered the booth.

The wind got hold of the frail structure and made it shake and tremble. The canvas walls now bulged outward, now pressed inward and pushed against the backs of the celebrants sitting inside. The boughs of the oak roof made a rumbling noise, swayed to and fro, and shook the clusters of grapes hanging down from them, so that the grapes dropped one after the other onto the table. The shadows of the men sitting around the table were projected onto the white sheets of the walls, and with the rise and fall of the candles' flames appeared as mystical, flickering images.

The believers looked at each other in silent anxiety. At the head of the table sat the Tzaddik, absorbed in the mysteries of the *Zohar*.

Suddenly he rose, and in a loud voice uttered the kabbalistic invitation:

"Heavenly guests, come, O come to my repast!"

The believers repeated after him:

"Heavenly guests, come, O come to our repast!"

Outside the wind whistled loudly, and the walls of the booth shook. The Tzaddik continued:

"Come, O Abraham our father, and after him Isaac, Jacob, Moses, Aaron, Samuel, Joseph, and David."

Suddenly complete darkness enveloped the booth. The storm tore off a branch from the roof, and the wind extinguished the candles.

A cold shiver seized the believers. All of them thought that they saw the heavenly guests, clad in white robes, enter and surround the chair of the Tzaddik.

For a moment there was deathly silence in the booth. Then the Tzaddik began to speak in the dark, and the wind gave his voice a peculiar, mystical timbre.

"'And the Lord God will blow the horn, and will go with the whirlwinds of the south.' Those who erect their ornate booths in massive stone houses do not feel the nearness of the Lord of Storms. The Feast of Booths is even more holy than the Day of Atonement. On this feast the Children of Israel, all as one, one in heart and one in soul, enter the booth of the Shekhinah."

The wind again shook mightily the walls of the darkened booth. The Tzaddik stopped speaking for a moment, and then continued in a low voice:

"On the Feast of Booths the heavenly visitors come. And happy is the eye that can see their snow-white color."

The believers looked around in the dark. The oak branches of the roof hummed, as if murmuring the secrets of the storm into the ears of the celebrants.

The Tzaddik continued:

"And happy is the ear that hears their softly speaking voice."

The believers sat silently, motionless, in the dark, as if they wanted to hear what the heavenly visitors were telling the Tzaddik about the judgment of the New Year.

Suddenly light spread throughout the booth. Lighted candles had been brought from the house.

The believers looked at each other in wonder, enraptured. Some of them glimpsed, in the first flash of light, the departure of a white old man. Was it Abraham, Isaac, or Jacob, or perhaps King David in his royal cloak?

The Tzaddik triumphantly intoned the words of the Psalm:

He concealeth me in His pavilion in the day of evil,
He hideth me in the covert of His tent.

And next day also the followers of the Rymanower carried their *etrogs* and *lulavs* into the synagogue as if they were symbols of triumphant achievement.

And on this feast nobody asked of those who returned from Berdichev to Rymanow where was the triumph.

——8——

The Saint Who Loved to Sing

ne Sabbath afternoon, at the Third Meal, in the mysterious dusk, when the Heavenly Channels open and wonderful visions pour down upon pure souls, the Tzaddik of Lublin said to the believers sitting around him:

"In the Land of Hungary a great luminary has arisen, a star of blinding brilliance, whose light derives from the seven days of Creation."

And the next day two believers set out to find the hidden star.

For a long time they wandered in the country, until finally they learned that the light they yearned for was shining in the town of Nagykálló. They therefore directed their steps there, and arrived in the little town on the day preceding Passover.

As they approached the court of the rabbi, their ears perceived song and music. They were astonished. Could it be that Purim in Nagykálló lasted until Pesah? They came nearer, and could discern the words of the song:

When Israel came out of Egypt,
The House of Jacob from among a foreign people . . .

"This is a Passover Psalm," thought the pilgrim Hasidim, and they entered the courtyard.

The whole house of the rabbi was in a turmoil. The Tzaddik of Kálló was baking his matzot, with the help of the men of his community. Outside, in the courtyard heaped high with firewood, the white-bearded talmudist Reb Hayyim Nahman was washing the dishes, which were changed every five minutes lest the dough sticking to their sides begin to ferment. Inside, in the room, Reb Hezkel the scribe was kneading the dough, his long black beard colored white by the dust of the flour. Around the long table the most honored members of the community worked with bent backs, stretching and flattening the lumps of dough distributed to them. Little boys, their faces framed by long earlocks, were bustling about, busily carrying the ready matzot to the puncturer, who ran his heavy nail-studded iron roller several times back and forth over the thin sheets of dough, so that they should not develop bubbles. Then they hurriedly took the matzot to the oven before which sat the Rabbi himself, in a white shirt with wide sleeves, and a little white cap on his head. The Tzaddik smilingly held out a long thin stave to the boys as they ran up to him, and they deftly lowered onto it the matzot from their rolling pins. The fire which radiated out through the open door of the oven lighted the shining face and high white forehead of the Tzaddik, pearled by glistening beads of perspiration. The slamming of the many rolling pins, the clanking of the puncturing iron, and the knocking of the firewood carried by the boys were all swallowed up by the singing of the working group, which, encouraged by the Tzaddik, became ever louder and louder. The songs were always intoned by the Tzaddik, and the rays of the melodies issuing from before the oven filled the room and spread beyond it, so that ultimately the whole house, the kitchen, and even the courtyard were bathed in the light of the songs. In a corner three Klezmer musicians accompanied the songs on violin, dulcimer, and flute.

> They say among the nations,
> God wrought miracles for us.

And the matzot were stretched under the rhythmical movements of the rolling pins, which spontaneously followed the beat of the music.

The foreign Hasidim stopped at the threshold, amazed at the sight. Never before had they seen anything like this.

It took Reb Hayyim Nahman, who was scraping the dishes with a feverish haste, several minutes to notice the two strangers. He quickly wiped his right hand, and stretched it out toward them in greeting.

"*Sholem aleikhem!* Peace be upon you! From where are you?"

"From Lublin."

"And where are you going?"

"We want to stay here with the Rabbi over Pesah."

"When did you leave home?"

The two strangers impatiently disregarded the question.

They wanted to see the Tzaddik, for whose sake they had undertaken the long journey.

"Where is now your Rabbi?"

Old Hayyim Nahman pointed with his thumb at the man who sat before the oven, and who just at that moment wiped the sweat from his brow with the white sleeve of his shirt.

"But he wears foreign clothes?" asked one of the Hasidim, surprised.

"Those are not foreign clothes," answered old Hayyim Nahman proudly. "It is a Hungarian apparel. At home our Rabbi often walks about in nothing but a shirt, of course a long white one, reaching to the ground, because at times his frail body cannot bear anything else. You should see him on those occasions! Adam must have been like him in the Garden of Eden before he sinned."

In the meantime, between one kneading of the dough and another, they interrupted work for a few minutes, and the believers formed a circle around the Tzaddik and all of them began to dance to the tune of a Psalm.

"Look, how beautifully he dances!" remarked one of the strangers.

"As if in his youth he had danced with maidens," added the other.

Reb Hayyim Nahman responded enthusiastically:

"You should see how he dances at weddings! He stands up before the gypsies, has the melodies played for him, and dances with such abandon that the assembled young people, the youths and the maidens, forget each other, and instead of sinning by joint dances they just stand and gaze at the Rabbi."

"That's why he does it," interjected another believer, who had in the meantime curiously approached the strangers.

At that moment the people inside broke out into a new song. But the words of this one were no longer from the Psalms of David, but from those sad Hungarian songs which the shepherds, cattle herds, and horsemen were used to singing around the campfire, under the open sky: "Csinom Palkó, Csinom Jankó."

The two strangers looked at each other, surprised. But Reb Hayyim Nahman explained to them that it was the custom of the Rabbi Kálló to sing Hungarian songs even on the most sacred holy days, because he said that the fate of the Hungarians was similar to that of the Jews.

When the baking of the matzot was finished, the Tzaddik rose, wiped the perspiration from his forehead, washed his face, and went outside. The believers thronged after him.

"The Tzaddik surely goes to the *mikveh*, the sacred bath," said the strangers, following in the footsteps of the others. "After all, the holiday is soon about to begin."

But they were mistaken. The Tzaddik directed his steps toward the fields outside the town. The trees had started to blossom already, and the rays of the sun shone through dense foliage onto the broad meadow, whose silken green carpet was speckled by purplish crocuses. The quiet of the sundrenched spring air was interrupted only by the song of birds and the pipe of a shepherd boy. The Tzaddik stopped in the middle of the field and thirstily inhaled the fresh spring scents:

"What a pleasure it is to bathe here in the air. What a pleasure to immerse the soul here in songs. This is the most sacred bath."

The little shepherd boy began to walk slowly homeward, and playing his reed passed near the Rabbi. The Tzaddik motioned him to approach:

"Come here, my son, and play that melody again for me," asked the Tzaddik in a gentle voice.

The boy was touched by the words, and repeated the air. The Tzaddik listened to it with pleasure. Then, looking deep into the eyes of the boy, he said:

"This is a sacred tune, my son. It is like the Song of Songs. Play it once more."

The little boy, as if he had become confused by the intense glance of the Tzaddik, tried to play it again, but was unable to. The melody seemed to have gotten stuck in the pipe. He started it several times, but all in vain.

"Well, give it to me," said the Tzaddik. He took the pipe from the boy and started to play the tune. The soft spring breeze subsided, the rustle of the boughs died down, the crocuses lifted their heads, and the birds squatted silently on the branches and listened with wide-open eyes to the melody played by the holy man.

Dusk fell. The Tzaddik, with tears in his eyes, returned the pipe to the boy, who was saddened by having forgotten the song. The Tzaddik started back, toward the synagogue.

When the Tzaddik led the Passover evening prayers, he sang them to the tune of the little shepherd boy's pipe. And as he stood there before the reading desk, all the believers hummed the melody with him, all the souls were filled with the new air, and the long, white candles seemed to move their flickering heads to the rhythm of the new song.

By the time the night had descended, the Night of Pro-

tection, in which the evil demons hide and only the soul of Elijah wanders among the houses of the Children of Israel, the house of the Tzaddik of Kálló was like an abode transformed by a miracle. Everywhere festive purity glittered. The table, on which as late as midday the hard rolling pins were still beating the thin dough, was covered with a white tablecloth, and on it were arranged many white settings. In the middle a big twelve-branched candlestick was burning, lighting up the face of the Tzaddik with a softer glow than the fire of the oven earlier in the day. Clad in festive white clothes, the Tzaddik sat at the head of the table, leaning back against the pillows of an easy chair. Around the table sat several visitors.

The Lubliner Hasidim waited impatiently to hear profound words of Torah or kabbalistic secrets from the lips of the Tzaddik. But in vain. The *Seder* night was almost finished, and they had heard nothing but songs and airs. Hebrew Psalms and Hungarian tunes alternated. The Tzaddik sang even the words of the Passover Haggadah to a wonderful, soft melody. Even for the story of the ten plagues of Egypt he had a deep, touching, sorrowful tune.

"Well, we surely came here in vain," thought the Lublin Hasidim, and no longer expected anything miraculous.

The clock struck midnight when the Tzaddik of Kálló reached the prayer for which in the houses of Israel the door is being opened so as to receive the visiting spirit of Elijah. The Tzaddik himself got up and opened the door leading to the street.

"Blessed be he who comes in the name of God!"

Barely did the words of welcome leave the lips of the Tzaddik when, to the surprise of those assembled, a peculiar, gaunt figure of an old peasant, clad in a white long sheepskin coat, with a shepherd's crook in his hand, appeared in the doorway. With eyes sunk deep into themselves he took a few stiff steps forward.

"Blessed be he who comes in the name of God!" repeated the Tzaddik. He took the visitor by the hand and led him to the table.

The people who sat around grew frightened. They were awed by the mysterious night visitor, and were apprehensive lest he touch the festive wine with his hands.

Without uttering a word, the old shepherd sat down next to the Tzaddik, then reached across the table to the big silver Cup of Elijah, brim full of wine, that stood in its middle.

"The Cup of Elijah! The Cup of Elijah!" The believers started up in alarm, and jumped up from their seats.

The old shepherd quickly drank up all the wine from the big cup and then rose, preparing to leave.

"Sing at least one beautiful song!" spoke the Tzaddik, who watched quietly what was happening, and enjoined silence on his followers.

The old shepherd gave no answer, but started to move toward the door. The Tzaddik repeated in an imploring tone of voice:

"Do not leave my house without a song!"

"Well then, so be it," spoke the old shepherd at long last, and his voice sounded as if it were from the Other World. "I shall sing your song, the one which you took today from the boy with the pipe and sanctified."

And he put his right hand on the shoulder of the Tzaddik:

"But you too must sing with me!"

And the Tzaddik and the shepherd together intoned the melancholy, sorrowful air:

The cock is crowing,
Soon it will be morning.
In the green forest,
In the blue meadow,
A bird is strolling.

What kind of a bird?!
What kind of a bird?!
Golden of beak, golden of legs,
For me it is waiting.

Wait, O bird, wait!
Wait, O bird, wait!
If God has destined me for you,
Soon yours I shall be.

All those sitting around the table and listening to the sad tune fell into a reverie, and did not notice when the mysterious shepherd suddenly disappeared.

And as for the Tzaddik, he repeated the melody quietly and sadly, with Hebrew additions about the rebuilding of the Temple and the city of Zion, and the coming of Redemption.

The cock is crowing,
Soon it will be morning.
Yibbaneh hamikdash, ir Tziyon temalle,[1]
When will that come to be?
Vesham nashir shir hadash uvirnana naaleh,[2]
It's time for it to be.

---

1. The Sanctuary will be rebuilt, the City of Zion will be filled.
2. And there we shall sing a new song and go up in jubilation.

When the two pilgrim Hasidim returned to Lublin, and recounted with great disappointment their experiences in Nagykálló, the Tzaddik of Lublin said with admiration:

"Nobody has ever been as close to the spirit of Elijah as the Kállóer. His soul has its roots in the Hall of Songs, and with him every sacred act becomes a song. It is with song and melody that he serves the Almighty, Who approaches him on the wings of songs to delight in His faithful holy servant."

9

The Talmudist Maiden

he whole world knows that the Tzaddik of Belz was chosen by heaven for the holy task of fulfilling the role of the Messiah and redeeming the world. His soul rose up to such heights of holiness and purity that even the angels of heaven looked upon him with envy. The joy-filled times of redemption were about to arrive, and all the sufferings of the world were to come to an end. But then Satan, for whom, as is well known, the suffering of man causes the greatest pleasure, interfered. The Evil One frustrated the divine plan for the world's salvation, and this is the sad story of how it happened.

*   *   *

In faraway White Russia, in sandy Lithuania, where the children, as we know, begin to study the Talmud while still in their cradle, and where, as is likewise known to everybody, the greatest talmudists of the world grow out of the *heders* and the yeshivot like grass in the field or the saffron of meadows, there lived a maiden who was so beautiful that no human tongue could describe her. The only one who, perhaps, could have done justice to her beauty was King Solomon, who knew how to sing the sacred Song of Songs about Shulamit, but even that he was able to do only because the divine spirit inspired him, and because Shulamit was not a flesh-and-blood Judean girl but the very soul of Israel, whose beloved was not an earthly prince but the King of Kings himself, blessed be His name.

As for this girl, not only was her beauty famous in lands near and far, but also her knowledge of the Talmud, even though women students of the Talmud were not at all rare in Lithuania. But this girl was a veritable female *gaon*. Ever since her earliest childhood a wondrous thirst for knowledge burned in her soul. All day long, from morning to evening, she stayed in her room with her little orphan brother, who was being taught by a great talmudic genius, and while the boy penetrated the secrets of the Talmud and the ancient holy writings, she too listened to the instruction and progressed, together with her brother, from stage to stage, higher and higher. And it happened more and more frequently that when the master asked a particularly exacting question, which the boy could no longer answer, she, with a prodigious ingenuity, solved the difficult problem. All the people of the city, young and old, scholars and ignorants, admired the beautiful talmudist maiden.

The fame of the phenomenal maiden soon spread from city to city, from village to village, until the whole land was filled with her name. Even in faraway foreign lands there were those who had heard about her.

The father of the maiden died, and left a rich estate for his two children. The boy waited until he reached the age of eighteen, and then, obeying the word of Scripture, married. The maiden remained alone, and continued to perfect her divine scholarship. And when she felt that she could measure her strength against the great ones, she set out on a long journey to get acquainted with the leading talmudists of the world. She traveled from city to city, and was everywhere received with great festivities. The greatest talmudists sought her out, entered into discussions with her, and admired the immeasurable depths of her knowledge. There was no question which she could not answer immediately, and when she asked a question the brightest talmudic luminaries stood silent before her.

The maiden's peregrinations led her to Belz, where she deeply desired to get acquainted with the world-famous great Tzaddik, the blazing torch of the Diaspora, whose holy light shone all over the world. But the Tzaddik, who had never in his life looked into the face of a strange woman, sent word to her that he did not want to talk to her, and even instructed his followers not to enter into conversation with her. As for his disciples, he strictly prohibited them from meeting the maiden.

"The pearls of the Talmud are not feminine jewels," he said to the students of the yeshivah. "Take care not to be led into temptation."

And the young men of the yeshivah carefully avoided meeting the strange maiden, and did not dare even to go near her. Only one youth, who had long been troubled by the thirst of knowing the answer to an especially difficult

brain-wracking problem, and in whom the love of the Torah was greater than the respect for the master's voice, went in secret to the maiden so as to present her with the inexplicable talmudic puzzle. The maiden easily solved the problem, and the youth hurried home radiant with joy. He did not breathe a word to the Tzaddik, but could not resist divulging the matter to one or the other of his fellow students. The young talmudists thereupon one by one stealthily sought out the maiden, put to her the questions that had been most bothersome to them, and came away happily with the answers, taking along with them also wondrous questions the maiden put to them, to ponder or to ask their master, the great Tzaddik, for the solutions.

Next day, when the Tzaddik met his students for talmudic instruction, several of them began to besiege him with questions of the deepest significance. The Tzaddik was struck with amazement. Never before had anybody addressed questions of such subtle acuity to him. When he thereupon began to question his students, they shamefacedly admitted that they had been unable to resist their urge to satisfy their thirst for knowledge, went in secret to visit the talmudist maiden, and it was she who put to them these questions, which were as deep as the sea and which, however much they wracked their brains, they were unable to answer.

"And did the beauty of the maiden not lead you into temptation?" asked the Tzaddik sternly.

"It is such a divine pleasure to hear the words of the holy Torah flow from her lips," answered the head of the class enthusiastically, "her radiant spirit soars into such heights, that no corporeal thought can arise in her presence."

The Tzaddik pondered, cogitated for a long time, and

searched the ancient books. But since even after three days he was still unable to answer the questions he had heard from his disciples, he too was filled with desire to hear the solutions.

"Go to her," he instructed his students at last, "and tell her to give you the answers to the questions she posed."

"But take care," the Tzaddik added softly, "take care that always at least two of you should be together with her, lest you transgress the prohibition of the sages, since it is forbidden to stay alone with a strange woman."

The youths returned sadly and informed the Tzaddik: the maiden sent word that she would give the answers only to the Tzaddik personally, since anyhow she had long yearned to make the acquaintance of the light of Israel, the shining beacon of the sea of the Talmud. If therefore the Tzaddik wanted to hear the explanations, let him receive her in his home.

For a long time the keen yearning for knowledge and the fear of the strange woman fought in the Tzaddik's heart. He had never before addressed words to a woman other than his spouse, and even to her only those that were most necessary. The sages said, "Do not multiply talk with a woman, not even with your wife, let alone with a stranger." But to delve into the secrets of the Torah was the greatest religious achievement. To understand a baffling passage, to pour content into a dead word, to penetrate the mysteries of the Sacred Scripture—this was the most sacred divine commandment. At the end, the love of the Torah was victorious in the Tzaddik's heart, and he let the maiden know that she should come to him, and that he was willing to listen in person to her answers.

When the maiden entered the big study of the Tzaddik,

his followers and the students of the yeshivah gazed enchanted at her unearthly beauty, and only the Tzaddik himself did not raise his eyes. He sat stiff and motionless in his place, and waited for the maiden to speak.

The voice of the girl sounded like a heavenly bell as she, with wondrous ease, solved the mysterious talmudic problems one after the other. The whole room became filled with the fiery air of the Torah, and nobody dared to interrupt with as much as a single word. The Tzaddik himself, as if he had fallen into a reverie under the influence of supreme pleasure, listened motionless to the presentation of the maiden, and only when she suddenly fell silent did he speak with a soft voice:

"You have not yet given, my daughter, the answer to the last question, even though it is the deepest, and the one I most wished to hear."

"That one answer," said the maiden, "since it is a matter for the greatest alone, I can only give if nobody else hears it."

Surprise swept over the whole room. The followers and the youths looked at one another questioningly. What would the Tzaddik now do?

But the soul of the Tzaddik was already totally submerged in the pleasures of the mysteries of the Torah, and he said, as if oblivious of himself:

"If so, let everybody leave!"

In a minute the big room of the Tzaddik was emptied, even though here and there voices of astonishment were heard.

"Isn't it forbidden to remain alone?" said one.

"The Torah gives protection," said his neighbor, pushing his way out.

And the Tzaddik remained alone with the strange maiden.

His thirsting lips imbibed eagerly the sacred mysteries that flowed from the lips of the wondrous maiden. Each of her words sounded like a song played on the heavenly harps of angels. His soul, his heart, his entire being resonated with a heavenly pleasure, and he could not restrain himself from looking up for a moment at the miraculous being from whose mouth issued the miraculous voice that enveloped him.

And as he looked at the wonderful beauty of the maiden, he felt for a moment that into the scent of the Torah which wafted from her lips was mixed the intoxicating balsamic breath of the maiden's mouth.

The Tzaddik shook with a sudden shudder. He rose, ran to the door, tore it open, and cried with a voice that was almost beseeching:

"My friends, my disciples, come in!"

* * *

And those who could see deeper into the course of the world knew that this whole matter was the work of Satan, who was able only with the power of the Torah to make the Tzaddik of Belz commit such a little sin, and thus prevent him from becoming the long-expected redeemer of the suffering world.

——10——

The Death of the Baal Shem

or several years prior to his death he was able only with great effort to hold back his soul from flying up to Heaven, to the Hall of Souls. Each time he intoned a prayer, and the wings of his soul began to unfold to take the supplications up into the Heights, the desire overcame him to rise through the Ten *Sefirot* to the Crown, and to reunite with its original source, the Divine Glory, from which it had issued in the beginning of the days. At such moments he would collapse, and the believers would watch terrified the convulsion of the pure body of the Tzaddik, lift him up, and place him gently upon his couch. But soon he would come to, and tell in a tremulous voice what visions had opened up to him while his soul was wandering On High.

Once his soul was almost torn out of his body forever. It was the eve of Yom Kippur, and even though the Tzaddik was very weak he insisted on leading in the *Kol Nidrei*

prayer, for he saw that the sentence that was about to be pronounced up above on the Children of Israel was very severe and merciless, and that had to be prevented. But scarcely had he uttered a few sentences, barely was he able to connect his thoughts with the First *Sefirah*, when his soul was attracted by the Infinite, it flew higher and higher, and when it reached that Hall he heard the souls whisper to each other, trembling with delight:

"The Baal Shem is coming! The Baal Shem will be among us!"

But the pure soul flew higher and higher, to merge with the rays of the radiant Crown. But then, On High, among the branches of the Tree of Life, from the Bird's Nest, a song reached it, the song of the soul of the Messiah . . . a song that attracted the soul of the Baal Shem irresistibly, and revealed to it that the sentence would be mitigated, but that the time of its ascent to Heaven had not yet come. It would have to return to earth and continue disseminating its teachings, the mysteries that purified the souls, for the time of Redemption could not arrive until all the souls were purified.

And the soul obeyed. The Baal Shem came to, and with an almost inaudible voice continued the *Kol Nidrei*. And the believers knew that the Baal Shem could not die on Yom Kippur, since he was free of sins.

Three days later, at the First Meal of the Sabbath, the Baal Shem spoke of the union of the soul and God, which was an infinitely greater pleasure than the union of bride and groom. And who was there among the believers who did not know that he had heard these mysteries at that time, in the Above?

His soul had to spend several more months on earth.

But those months were full of mercy and fecundity. The Tzaddik no longer left his room, and the believers always surrounded him and listened to his words. All week long he spoke only a little, but at the Third Meal of the Sabbath, at dusk, which was neither day nor night, he always revealed great mysteries. And happy was he who could hear them.

"Scripture says, 'The earth is full of His glory.' Everything is full of God, and God is in everything, even in the evil desires, in the sinful acts. But the sin causes him pain—this is the suffering of the Shekhinah. However, many times He hides. Look, out there it is cold already, the leaves are fallen, the flowers have faded, the birds are silent, and the little brook is frozen over. For the King has gone into hiding, the Court has moved away, and with it also joy, happiness, and light are gone. But He can go into concealment only from the trees, the flowers, the birds, and the brook, for they have no thought. Man, however, can imagine Him, his soul can always conjure Him up, and that which lives in the thought is true life, and only that which lives in our thoughts does truly live. It is thought that unites the soul with the Supernal, and therefore one must always be joyful, for it is unseemly to sorrow in front of the King. We can step before His countenance only with joy in the heart."

The Baal Shem lived to see the return of the King and his court, when warm sunlight filled his chamber, which was set up to serve as his prayer room. But his body grew ever weaker, and only through the window could he enjoy the sights of the holiday, only behind the window was he able to recite silently the prayer greeting the flowers.

Still, festive serenity hovered over the room. And when

the Great Sabbath arrived, the one preceding Passover, the great day on which all blessings are doubled and all the divine Channels become filled, one could read in the countenance of the Tzaddik that the Mercy of Mercies was near, and everyone waited with anticipation for the Third Meal of the Sabbath.

"The whole world is but song and dance before the Supernal One. The universe is all song, and everyone and everything adds a note to it. Every soul is a musical note, and every letter of the Torah is a musical note, and every soul is a letter of the Torah. And the greatest pleasure of the note is to melt smoothly and sweetly into the Great Song which cheers the King and induces Him to mercy. The soul merges into the song when it flies out of the body, and therefore its greatest joy is to be granted to take leave of the body on the day of the Giving of the Torah, for on that day the universe is full of the myrrh-scented letters of the Torah."

This is what the Tzaddik said at the Third Meal. And he who had an ear to hear and an eye to see could know for certain that the Baal Shem would take leave of the earthly world on the Feast of Revelation.

The Tzaddik himself was thereafter merry and joyful all the time. A sweet excitement shone from his face, as if he were preparing for a wonderful voyage. And when, between Pesah and Shavuot, he counted the days of the *Omer*, though his voice became weaker and weaker, he recited the prayer with increasing enthusiasm. He was filled with an infinite joy that only a few days were separating him from the goal, and that those days diminished all the time. Five days, four days, three days, two days, one day.

On the eve of Shavuot, when the Bride puts on her most

splendid raiments and her most sparkling jewels to be
clothed in the most intoxicating beauty when accepting
from the Groom the most wonderful wedding present, the
Torah, on that night, when Bar Yohai and the Company
descend to the earth to spread the blinding light of the
Kabbalah far and wide, the Baal Shem, dressed in a snow-
white festive robe, stood before the Holy Ark covered with
flowers and wreathes. There he recited the prayer, and from
the Ark petals of fragrant flowers and leaves fell upon his
head and shoulders. The Torah crowned him with a gar-
land for his great voyage.

After prayer he suddenly paled and began to reel. A
believer quickly approached him, and he leaned on his
shoulder and with slow trembling steps went to his couch.
He lay down. The multitude of candles burning on the
table shed a wonderful light on the white figure of the
Tzaddik, on his white locks, white beard, and white garb.
Out of the pure whiteness only two black flames radiated,
the black, blazing eyes of the Tzaddik.

The alarmed believers surrounded the couch of the
Tzaddik and searched his countenance anxiously.

One of them burst into tears and fell on his knees next
to the couch.

"Master, do not leave us!"

The Tzaddik raised his eyes and said:

"Do not say that. I am not leaving you. I go out one door
and return through the other. But there too I shall always
be with you. I am not leaving you."

The eyes of the believers filled with tears. His devoted
disciple, the youth of Mezhirech, began to sob loudly:

"My Master, it is the day of the Giving of the Torah. On

this day you were wont to shed light into the darkest recesses. Open now too your lips to reveal sacred mysteries."

The Tzaddik raised his hand and placed it on the head of the youth:

"Be blessed, you young torch. From now on you will spread light into the world."

The glances of the believers turned for a moment toward the wondrous youth; then they continued to listen to the barely audible words of the Tzaddik:

"I have not much time left. But one mystery still I want to reveal to you. Scripture says, 'The righteous liveth in his faith.' But I am telling you that also he who is not righteous lives in his faith . . . because he believes in his denial. . . . Faith is the main thing. There must be faith."

Suddenly the head of the Tzaddik fell back, his eyes closed, but a few seconds later opened again:

"They are coming for me. Open the door. Bar Yohai and the Company have descended from heaven. They want to come to me. Open the door. Welcome, Bar Yohai. Welcome, you miraculous Light. Sit down here next to me, sit down all of you, you holy masters who are intoxicated with the light of Glory. Soon we shall go."

The Tzaddik again closed his eyes for a moment. Then he spoke again, with a voice fainter and fainter:

"Look, there come the wandering, errant souls. They come from all corners of the world. They have wandered so long, and were not allowed to go up before the Throne. Now they come so that I should take them along. Come, you errant, orphan souls. Your sins are forgiven. Come, I shall take you to the Source of Light."

Suddenly the voice of the Tzaddik faltered. With a trem-

bling hand he clutched at his heart, and a moment later he whispered in a barely audible voice:

"My soul is preparing for the journey. It takes leave of the body. It slowly bids farewell to the husk which was its holy abode. Now it says good-bye to the heart. Now it takes leave of the hand."

The hands of the Tzaddik drooped.

"Now it bids farewell to my eye. Open the Holy Ark! I want to see the Torah with my last glance."

The youth of Mezhirech ran to the Holy Ark, pulled aside the curtain, and opened its door. The believers all turned in that direction, and from their feverish lips, in unison, as if uttered by a single voice, up rose the words of the petition:

"Our Father, our King! Open the gates of heaven to our prayers!"

The eyes of the Tzaddik slowly closed. But from his lips one could still hear the words:

"Now my soul takes leave of my lips. It is difficult for it to separate from my lips. It kisses them, kisses them, with endlessly sweet kisses. It is hard for it to take leave. Look, a flaming pillar of fire is descending from heaven. The Divine Matron is coming. The Shekhinah. It is taking my soul in a kiss. Come."

The youth of Mezhirech broke sobbing into the prayer for the dead. And the door of the Holy Ark closed.

——11——

The Tzaddik Who Craved the Messiah

very midnight, when the big clock on the wall chimed twelve times, the Tzaddik of Ujhely, Rabbi Moses son of Hannah, shook nervously, raised his head from the big folio, and looked around sadly:

"He hasn't come yet?"

None of the believers who stood about him answered his question. The Tzaddik suddenly rose from his armchair, went to the window, leaned out, and with his sorrowful, big eyes gazed for a long time into the silent, dark night. Then he went with tottering steps to the door, opened it, looked out, and closed it again.

"He has not yet come," he repeated dolefully.

For a moment he remained standing next to the door, then, as if resigning himself to the will of the Almighty, he touched with his lips the name of God that shone toward him out of the capsule of the Holy Writ nailed to the doorpost. Then he stepped up to the hearth, took out a handful of ashes, and spread them on his forehead, on the spot where for the morning prayers he was wont to put the sacred *tefillin*, while he murmured silently the words of the prophet:

> To appoint unto them that mourn in Zion,
> To give unto them a garland for ashes.

Dispiritedly he took off his shoes, washed his hands, and sat down on the floor, next to the door. He placed on the wooden footstool the wax candle that was mystically flickering in the dark corner next to him. He bent his head deep down to his knees, and beating his breast he recited the *Oshamnu*, the confession of sins, and then, sobbing, intoned the midnight prayer:

> By the waters of Babylon, there we sat and cried
> Remembering Zion.

He sobbed throughout as he recited the midnight songs about murderous Edom and suffering Jerusalem, about the blood that cries from the depths of the earth to high heaven, the unburied bodies of the dear children that lie around the Holy City and are being devoured by the birds of prey, and about the unhappy mother, Rachel, who wanders disconsolate on the heights of Ramah, and cries bitterly over her exiled and lost children.

> Gather together, ye children of Jacob, and hear,
> And rend your heart, not your garments.
> Because of your sins your mother was exiled.

And the song of bitter mourning sings of the Shekhinah, the Light of God, who herself wanders in exile, crying and calling for her Spouse, for she has no one who can comfort her. She is the Soul of Israel, whose beauty once radiated like that of an eternal Bride on Mount Zion, under the baldachin of the Clouds of Glory, but who now drags herself about like a beggar woman, cast out into the street, with the garments torn off by the enemy, and she is forsaken and unspeakably miserable. And the sad song speaks of the Torah, who too mourns ever since her glory was desecrated, and whose crown fell when her holy sanctuary became the prey of flames.

For more than an hour the Tzaddik of Ujhely sat on the floor and cried and shed his tears. When he reached the words of Consolation, he suddenly rose and, as if his heart had been filled anew with confidence, he sang in a jubilant tone:

> Shake thyself from the dust,
> Arise, O captive Jerusalem;
> Loose thyself from the bands of thy neck,
> O captive daughter of Zion.

The believers, who had sat in hushed silence around the table, now joined the Tzaddik in song and hand clapping, and at that moment they felt the truth of what the Tzaddik of Kálló had said, that the soul of the Prophet Jeremiah had arisen again in their Rabbi, and that is why he could mourn the destruction of Jerusalem with a heart as full of pain as if he had seen it with his own eyes, and that is why he awaited so impatiently, day and night, the coming of the Messiah and the rebuilding of Zion.

Only a few hours were left of the night, and the Tzaddik retired into his sleeping cubicle:

"Stay on the lookout, and if you hear any noise in the night wake me instantly, for surely the Messiah is coming!"

The believers sat awake in turns all night in the neighboring room. The Tzaddik rested on his couch with half closed eyes, and jumped up at the slightest noise:

"Has he come?" he asked, as if half asleep, and then fell back on his resting place.

At the first streak of dawn the Tzaddik was already awake. He washed his hands and face, and then hurried to the window and opened it.

Like shining little angels the rays of dawn sneaked into the steamy room and filled it with light, with glitter.

The Tzaddik spread out his arms toward the open sky, and in a sweetly melodious voice recited the greeting of the dawn. Then he turned to his believers:

"He has not yet come. But my right ear constantly hears the sound of the Messiah's trumpet, while the song of the heavenly hosts reverberates in my left ear. He has not yet come, but he will come! If not today, surely tomorrow!"

All day long the Tzaddik was busy with the affairs of his believers, who from near and far made the pilgrimage to him, some with complaints, others with requests, some for advice, others for help. Rabbi Moses listened to all of them, patiently, gently. He gave advice, he comforted, he encouraged, he strengthened the hands of the weak, poured new life into the broken hearts. All the while he occasionally sighed:

"Lord of the Universe! Lift the earthly worries from the

shoulders of Your children, so that all of them will be pure like the angels of heaven, and then Redemption can come!"

When Pesah, the Feast of Liberation, neared, the Tzaddik could no longer curb his impatient expectation of the Messiah. Already in the early afternoon he put on his festive clothes, put six pieces of matzot in a basket, and next to them a bottle of wine and a big silver cup. He tied the basket to his staff, hung it over his shoulder, and stood in front of the window, on the lookout, and listening whether he could hear the blast of the Messiah's trumpet. Thus he stood, gazing into the distance, until it grew dark. And when his followers gently reminded him that the time for the festive prayers had arrived, and that the people were waiting for him in the synagogue, he sadly put down the basket and said in a discouraged tone:

"He is still not coming! But perhaps there still are souls which must first become cleansed, so that they should be able to go with the Redeemer, so that they should not remain in eternal damnation. Let us then wait a little longer for them, since they too are our brothers!"

Thus passed day after day, year after year. And the Tzaddik of Ujhely expected the Messiah every moment. His beard, his hair had become white, his eye clouded over, time ploughed deep furrows into his forehead and face, his back became bent, his limbs grew weak. Only by leaning on the shoulders of two young men from among his followers was he able to take a few steps in his room. And Rabbi Moses was very troubled that perhaps now the Messiah would come, and how could he follow his triumphal carriage that would come tearing along? But then he became comforted by the words of the ancient holy sages,

who said that when the Messiah comes the Lord will take
the sun out of its case, so that it can spread its light freely
upon the earth, the evil ones will perish from the powerful rays, but the righteous ones will be healed and rejuve-
nated. And for a moment the Tzaddik felt as if the sacred
words had already come true for him and he had regained
his youthful strength. He rose from his chair, but barely
did he take a few steps when he sank on his couch, bereft
of all strength.

And Rabbi Moses son of Hannah felt that his last hour
was nigh. A deadly disease ravaged his weak body, which
was close to total collapse. But all the pain of his body was
overshadowed by the infinite anguish of his soul that he
would not live to see the coming of the Messiah. His eyes
became inflamed from excitement and yearning, and his
wrinkled forehead was covered with feverish beads of perspiration. The believers stood around the snow-white sick-
bed with bent heads, with heavy hearts, and silently murmured Psalms, looking with anxiety at the dying holy man.

Suddenly the silent recital was interrupted. The Tzaddik
raised his head, sat up in his bed, and lifting his arms toward heaven, cried:

"Master of the Universe! My Creator, my Father! I am
the smallest of Your servants, but You know that nothing
but the truth has ever been spoken by my mouth. Now,
too, I cannot lie. I must tell You that which burns in my
heart. My Creator, My Father! Had Your servant, Moses
son of Hannah, known that he would grow old and white,
and the Messiah would not come, he surely could not have
stood it. But You, Lord of the Universe, inveigled him
cunningly, day after day, until the poor man grew grey and
hoary. For the Lord of the Universe, it surely is an easy

thing to mislead such a poor fool. But at least now, let the Messiah come. Not for my sake, but for the sake of Your Name, so that it be sanctified on earth. I am not thinking of myself, You see my soul. But let me be the atoning sacrifice for all Israel. Let me not rise up to heaven, into the shining hall of the saints. Only let the Messiah come, and I shall sacrifice the salvation of my soul for the glory of Your Holy Name."

And Rabbi Moses fell back on his couch and gave up his pure soul.

And the pure soul wandered in the infinity of heavens for a long, long time. For the soul of Rabbi Moses did not want to enter the heavenly realm until the Messiah came on earth, and the time of the Redemption of all souls arrived. The soul of the Tzaddik fluttered about in the infinity of space, and they were unable to catch it and take it into the Hall of Souls, where the prophets, Moses and Jeremiah, waited for him longingly.

And then the heavenly hosts again resorted to a ruse. They sent down King David from his heavenly throne to approach the wandering soul of the Tzaddik. King David descended to the lower heavens, with the sound of harp and psaltery, and the song of Psalms. The soul of the Tzaddik flew in pursuit of the sweet sound of the harp and the enchanting song. Intoxicated by the music of the spheres, his soul rose higher and higher, attracted by the heavenly sounds. Until finally, awakening from its daze, it found itself in the Hall of Souls, where the souls of the saints sing their songs of consolation to the Lord, who every night rises from the Place of Concealment, and, bemoaning His unredeemed, suffering children, lets two great tear drops fall into the endless Ocean.

──12──

The Prayer of the Flute

ou of course think that the more you pray the better!" said our master Reb Shaye one day, when, coming from the synagogue, we arrived a little late in the *heder.*

And right away, fired by his thoughts, he continued:

"If you would only know what vicissitudes, what perilous roads await every word of prayer once it is uttered, before it can reach its distant goal! And, verily, I tell you, children, that often it is better not to pray."

We waited with bated breath, with eager curiosity, for the explanation of the master's words. And Reb Shaye was not tardy in enlightening us.

"Imagine, my sons, how much strength the prayer needs for nothing more than breaking through the ceiling of the synagogue in order to be able to fly up freely toward heaven! Once the Baal Shem—may he be our intercessor before the Throne of the Lord!—in the course of his wan-

derings came to the synagogue of a little town, but when
he reached the threshold, he stopped, frightened, as if his
feet were nailed to the ground. The believers asked him
timidly why he did not enter. And the Tzaddik—listen to
this!—answered that he could not enter because the synagogue was crowded with prayers. The local people were,
of course, glad to hear this, because they thought it was
flattering to their community, since, after all, every synagogue should be filled with prayers. But the Baal Shem
explained to them that in truth it was a great shame. For
those prayers which were uttered there did not stem from
the deepest depths of the soul, and therefore did not have
enough strength to break through the ceiling, and got
stuck between the walls of the synagogue. With time the
room became so overcrowded with them that it was impossible to enter the synagogue without treading on prayers.

"After repeated and fervent entreaties, the Tzaddik
nevertheless entered the synagogue, and the requests that
issued from his pure heart took along with them into the
Heights of Heaven also the prayers that were stuck down
below.

"But the Baal Shem does not appear every day," continued Reb Shaye. "And the number of prayers increases day
by day, the synagogues and prayer rooms become filled
up with them. At first they flutter here and there like white
little birds in a cage. Slowly, however, the space becomes
tighter and tighter, they must contract more and more, and
confined to one spot they hover sadly overhead. Then they
are forced to gather their wings, they whirl about in a great
clutter in the air, many of them collide and fall to earth,
wounded, in a swoon. And when we enter the synagogue

we tread on them, and the poor prayers moan and groan, cry and sob, but not everyone can hear them."

"I have heard them!" interrupted Rivele, who at the time of the study was wont to gaze into the distance with his big blue eyes. "Yes, indeed, I have heard them!"

The master sent a loving, soft glance at Rivele, and we looked at the kind face of Reb Shaye, and all of us were united in one wish: if only we would reach the degree where we could see the hovering prayers, the little white birdlings.

The master continued:

"And once the prayer breaks through the ceiling, how many dangers await it until it can pass the seven heavens and reach the Throne of God! Hosts of evil spirits and satans block its way at the entrance to each heaven; they drive it, pursue it, frighten it, and if the human heart has not poured into it enough strength, the prayer, alas, often falls back to earth. Or, if there is as much as a tiny blemish on its wings, a tiny blemish that got attached to it from an alien thought, it can no longer reach the Throne. And were it not for the good spirits who take them under their protection, few prayers could get there. But the good spirits hover there at the gates of the heavens, and often they engage in a quarrel, in a fight, with the demons over a prayer: they tear it from the talons of the demons, and fly up with it directly to the Hall of Glory, where all the prayers of millennia surround the splendidly shining Shekhinah in a flood of light."

"And if the Hall of Glory fills up, what will happen then?" asked Rivele the dreamer.

"Then the time of Mercy will arrive, the Messiah will

come, and all prayers will cease, because everyone will be happy, infinitely happy," replied Reb Shaye.

Then he returned to his subject:

"And the prayer, to be able to reach those heights, does not necessarily have to consist of words. Once the Baal Shem wandered for three days in a dense forest, sunk in solitude. He enjoyed the scent of the trees, the song of the birds, and this enjoyment was his prayer during those three days. And that is a much more sacred service of God than praying with words. That is the purest, disembodied prayer. The Levites in the Temple of Jerusalem used to play the harp, the drum, the flute, the zither, on the Sabbaths and the holy days, and that music was their prayer. The swishing of the raiment of the High Priest, the tinkling of the silver bells attached to the edge of his robe were a purer prayer than the words uttered by his mouth. The sound of the *shofar* on the day of Rosh Hashanah takes with it more prayers into heaven than the supplications of a thousand Tzaddiks . . . And the unselfish study of the divine teachings even more! Only in it can one achieve the highest degree of prayer."

The old clock on the wall struck nine. Reb Shaye stopped speaking, opened the great folio and leaned upon it with both hands. Then he took off his hat and put it on the table next to him. Under the hat he wore a little black velvet cap, which was all he kept on when he was teaching. We too opened our books and waited for the sign Reb Shaye was to give to one of us to begin the recital of the lesson. But the master could not tear himself away from the subject:

"It is late already, but there is still one story I want to tell you before I forget it.

"There lived in a village a poor Jewish husbandman who

used to spend the holy days always with the Baal Shem. He had a son whom it was impossible to get to learn anything. The boy would sneak away from school and wander about days on end in the fields and meadows and forests, playing his flute. Finally his father made him the shepherd of his flock of sheep. The boy reached the age of thirteen and still was not able to pray. But since the day of his *bar mitzvah* happened to fall on Yom Kippur, his father took him along to synagogue of the Baal Shem, so that he should at least hear the prayers of others.

All morning the boy sat silently next to his father. But when the believers recited the Silent *Mussaf*, he tugged sullenly at his father's coat:

"Father, I want to play my flute."

The father did not answer but silently continued his prayer. The boy waited until his father finished praying. When he saw that his father took the three steps back which signaled the end of his prayer, he spoke again:

"Father, I would like to play my flute!"

The father looked at him angrily:

"You brought along your flute to the synagogue? Don't you know that it is forbidden even to touch it on the holy day?"

The boy fell silent, and shamefacedly cast down his eyes. But a few hours later, when the time came for the Silent *Minhah* prayer, his face went red, and he began again to pull at his father's tallit:

"Father I want very much to play my flute!"

The father looked at him, and made an angry motion with his hand, as if he were threatening the boy with a beating. But he could not take the flute away from him, since on the holy day it was forbidden to touch it.

The boy flinched, but in his eyes a wild fire was burning, like the sacrificial fire on a sacred altar. His face had a red glow, and his forehead shone, glistened. And his father, seeing that the boy yearned so much to play the flute, was afraid lest he actually start playing it and cause a great consternation in the synagogue. When he finished his prayer, he asked the boy:

"In which of your pockets do you have the flute?"

"In this one, here."

And the boy lifted the wing of his jacket to the father. The father grabbed it strongly, so that the boy should not be able to take it out. This is how he began to recite the Silent *Neilah* prayer.

The whole congregation was praying silently, devotedly. Suddenly the boy gave a strong tug, pulled the wing of his jacket out of his father's hand, ran up to the reader's desk, and began to play his flute in loud abandon.

Great consternation seized the whole assembly. All of them looked toward the reader's desk, and from all sides one could hear cries of "Hush! Hush!" more and more angrily. More than that they could not say, because the *Neilah* must not be interrupted. And the boy stood there, with a flaming face, rooted to the spot, and played his tune on and on. No one could move from his place during the prayer, but threatening fists were raised toward the platform.

However, at that moment, to the great astonishment of all, the Baal Shem, who usually remained immersed in the *Neilah* prayer for a long time, took three steps backward, and then went straight up to the platform, embraced the boy, and planted a long, loving kiss on his forehead.

He stayed there, holding the boy in his embrace, until

all the people concluded their prayer. Then he said to the amazed believers, who rushed up and thronged around the platform:

"This little Tzaddik helped the prayers of all of us to rise up into heaven. That is why I too shortened the *Neilah*. He cannot recite prayers, but when he listened to the prayers offered by the Children of Israel on this holy day, he too was overcome by the yearning to pour out his soul before God. And as he could not express his flaming desire in words, he could quench the thirst of his soul only by playing his flute. And since his father prevented him all day long from fluting, the desire became more blazing, it ate out his heart more and more, and when it finally broke out in full force the prayer of his flute flew straight up to Heaven, into the Hall of Glory, to the throne of the Shekhinah, and it took along with it the prayers of all of us, also my prayer."

"This is what I wanted to tell you," Reb Shaye concluded his story. "I wanted you to have an idea about what true prayer was. And now, let us get down to studying!"

And we turned to our study with the full devotion of our young souls. For now we knew that pure, unselfish study was also a prayer.

——13——

Mayerl

ou, of course, ask, who is this Mayerl? And you don't notice that this question in itself is a big insult. Mayerl must be known to everyone, believers and opponents alike. Even the Lubliners, who so often like to mention that it was the Tzaddik of Lublin who made Mayerl great, recognize that he did become great. In fact, very great, as was foreseen by the far-reaching glance of the Lubliner.

Because Mayerl, before he "revealed himself" in Przemysl, used to make the pilgrimage to the Tzaddik of Lublin on every holy day, and thus got to learn by observing one thing and another, which the believers of Przemysl of course insist on denying. But even for that observation extraordinary powers were required, and happy is he who already in his youth can rise to the degree of being able to learn something from the Lubliner by observation.

When Mayerl first came to Lublin, he instantly attracted

the attention of the Tzaddik. Friday evening, after the prayer, he turned to the believers and asked:

"Who is that man who can beseech God so sweetly that even the angels of evil are touched by his entreaty?"

Of course, nobody could answer the Tzaddik's question. They left the synagogue, and all of them went to the house of the Tzaddik to greet the Sabbath there too. But barely was the first song finished when the Tzaddik asked again:

"Who is it who can sing so sweetly about Queen Sabbath, that even the heavenly accusers fall silent and listen to his song?"

Again, no one answered. But when at the *Kiddush*, the sanctification of the Sabbath, each of them held in his hand the wine cup to welcome the Queen, the Tzaddik of Lublin looked around with his big, fiery eyes, and noticed that at the foot of the table the wine in the cup of a young man was boiling up to such an extent that it ran over and dripped on the hand of his neighbor.

"What is your name, young man?" asked the Tzaddik of Lublin.

"Mayerl," answered the youth, turning red.

"From where are you?"

"From Przemysl."

"What are you?"

"Nothing."

"On what do you subsist?"

"On nothing."

"Come, sit here next to me."

And, as is well-known, he whom the Tzaddik of Lublin bids to sit next to him will sit next to him not only on this earth, but also in the Other World.

Many times thereafter Mayerl continued to come to Lublin. He had inherited from his father a little cart drawn by one horse, and on it he made his regular pilgrimages on the holy days. Once he wanted to spend the Hanukkah at Lublin to see how the Tzaddik lighted the sacred candles for the Feast of the Maccabees. It was a harsh winter. The snow lay knee-deep all over, and on the road one could frequently encounter wolves. Mayerl drove the horse joyfully, singing Psalms and Hebrew songs. As he was driving through the big forest between Przemysl and Lublin, he encountered an old Jew.

"From where are you coming?" asked Mayerl.

"From Lublin."

"And where are you going?"

"To Przemysl."

"Why are you going there?"

"I am giving away my daughter in marriage, and I must collect a few florins for the dowry."

"But if you walk like this, on foot, it will take you a very long time to get there. Can you drive a horse?"

"Yes."

"Well then, get up here on the cart, turn it around, and drive back. I can as well walk; my business is not urgent."

And Mayerl insisted in his offer, until the old man agreed and amidst deep sighs climbed up on the cart. As he was taking up the reins and started to drive off, Mayerl called after him:

"Wait a moment, old man! Sitting on the cart you can easily catch cold. Here is my coat, put it on. I shall be walking and thus shall keep warm."

The old man was touched to tears. He thought the miracle-working Elijah had appeared to him in the snowstorm. Mayerl continued on his way, on foot, in his thin cloak. In the heavy snowfall he got lost and wandered about all night in the forest. Only next morning did he reach Lublin, half frozen. When the Tzaddik of Lublin saw him, he scolded him in front of all the believers:

"Why are you still coming to me? Stay at home and wait for the people who will come to *you*."

From that moment on Mayerl became *Reb* Mayerl. On the way back he was accompanied by many believers, and soon the Tzaddik of Przemysl outdid even the Lubliner in some things.

The ways of Reb Mayerl were very different from those of all other Tzaddiks. He was called "The Merry Tzaddik." He was always joyful, was always singing, and his face was always shining. "What God orders is always good, one must be glad to have it, whether it looks like a blessing or like a blow." People came to him from all over, with all kinds of requests, with troubles, with complaints, but when they saw the merry countenance of Reb Mayerl, no one dared to sadden him. And the joyfulness of Reb Mayerl affected also the believers: they forgot, or kept silent about, their complaints, and returned home cheered up, filled with new strength, new confidence. And if somebody nevertheless began to present his complaint to Reb Mayerl, he shouted at him:

"You deserved it because you are sad. Sadness is the greatest sin. The whole world rejoices, the earth rejoices, the heavens rejoice, the sun too rejoices, and the little stalks of grass too rejoice. In the winter, when the snow covers them, they rejoice in their sleep. Don't you see, everything rejoices, and the Shekhinah is present only where there is joy!"

Every afternoon Mayerl would go out into the forest and play hide-and-seek with the children. And if, in the course of playing, one of them called him "Rebbe," he stepped up to the child, stroked his head, and said to him with a smile:

"Call me Mayerl, don't be afraid. You are a greater 'Rebbe' than I. You have as yet no sin, only take care to remain free of sins later as well."

And everyone knows that those children with whom Reb Mayerl would play grew up to be great men.

But Mayerl played not only with children, but with God as well. His prayers were sweet songs, and otherwise, too, he would speak to his Creator as a boisterous child would to his parent. If something hurt him very much, he would fold his arms, look spitefully up to heaven, and begin to quarrel with God:

"Is it that You want, my Father, that I should sin against You? You can do with me whatever You want. Mayerl will remain Mayerl!"

And he was ready to enter into an argument with his Heavenly Father not only in his own interest, but also in that of others. Especially in the interest of sinners, who got into trouble. On such occasions he would slam his hand down on the table and cry angrily:

"Are You not ashamed, Lord of the Universe? You created man of flesh and blood, all feeble materials, and made him susceptible to every kind of sin, whereas You could have made him strong and firm, so that nothing should be able to make him swerve. And You do let him sin, even though You could have protected him—and now You even punish him? Are You not ashamed?!"

The words of Reb Mayerl had, of course, a great effect in heaven, and he achieved more with his wrangling than many another Tzaddik with his prayer.

Often, however, there was indignation On High that Reb Mayerl interfered in heavenly matters, and not merely requested but demanded. But Reb Mayerl could not be caught out. He would look up into the Heights roguishly:

"What is it You want, my sweet Father? I know that despite everything You love Mayerl."

But once the altercation became serious, and Mayerl came very near to losing his share in the World to Come.

This is what happened.

There lived in Przemysl a Jew by the name of Shime Bash, who made a living by informing on his brethren, and got much money for his denunciations. He caused many Jews to be imprisoned, deprived many women and children of their provider, and reduced many families to beggary. He lived a godless life, and when people saw him on the street they avoided him. They even considered it a great sin to exchange as much as a single word with him.

One evening, as Reb Mayerl was walking in the street with several of his followers, they encountered Shime Bash. Reb Mayerl stepped up to him, and stretched out his arms as if he wanted to stop him from continuing on his way. Shime Bash looked at him angrily:

"What does the Rebbe want of me?"

"I want to tell you," answered Reb Mayerl, "that you will have a share in the World to Come!"

"The Rebbe is mocking me," the informer snarled at him. "And it is dangerous to make fun of Shime Bash!"

"It is not a joke. Reb Mayerl is always merry, but he never

mocks anybody. I am telling you again, you will have a share in the World to Come."

Shime Bash was taken aback. He looked about hesitatingly, and asked with sadness:

"In the World to Come? I? I, who ruined so many Jewish families, who desecrated all the Sabbaths, all the holidays? I, with whom no Jew will exchange even a word?"

"You will get to the Other World," repeated Reb Mayerl. "I know it for sure, you will get to the Other World!"

Shime Bash turned pale. For a while he was unable to utter a word. Then his eyes flashed, as if something very strange had come to his mind, and, gazing harshly at Reb Mayerl, he asked:

"Rebbe, is it really sure that I shall get to the Other World?"

"I swear to you upon my own share in the World to Come!" answered Reb Mayerl.

The face of Shime Bash flared up. He turned around, and ran off. And the believers noticed that for hours on end he roamed about in the streets, as if unhinged or deranged, and then, with his head bent low in contrition, he entered the big synagogue.

And as for Reb Mayerl, for a long time he looked up into the Heights with eyes that seemed to penetrate the heavens, and then, suddenly, in an outburst of exultation, he began to dance and to clap his hands. After he quieted down, he turned to the astonished believers:

"Do you know why Mayerl is so happy? Not because of that one soul who repented. Sooner or later every soul returns to the Father of souls, who receives joyfully His erring children. Mayerl now rejoices over something else. Up in the Heights the heavenly family became very indignant that I promised a share in the World to Come to a notorious sinner before he atoned for his many sins. But I rendered an oath about it. That is, I pronounced the sentence that the gates of heaven will be opened for the sinner. But I, I am losing my share in the World to Come, upon which I swore. And this is why Mayerl is so happy. Mayerl is very happy because now he will serve God totally unselfishly, out of pure love. Do you understand? I shall serve my Father out of pure love, without expecting any reward in the Other World."

The evening fell, and Reb Mayerl went to the synagogue. Never before had they heard such a sweet prayer issue from his lips. Every sentence had a mysterious melody, which bathed the souls in an infinite pleasure. The melodies filled the synagogue, and everyone felt that great miracles were about to happen.

But after the prayer Reb Mayerl addressed the believers sadly:

"They do not want in heaven that I should serve my Creator in this manner. I was able to pray thus only once, and I felt that having reached this grade everything I requested would be fulfilled. But already they pronounced a new sentence in heaven. Because I was so happy to be able to serve God unselfishly, without expecting any reward, my share in the World to Come was restored to me. What a pity, what a pity! My God, if only I could have prayed more often in this manner!"

And the believers regretted even more that Reb Mayerl could not remain "on that grade." He was great anyway, they said, he did great things, and how much more he could have done on that grade!

—14—

There Was Once a Dog

he courtyard of the death house was already crammed with people. Among the women and children one could also see a few men hustle and fidget. They pushed close to the window, peeped in with sidelong glances, and shrank back with a shudder.

"What an ugly corpse!"

"As ugly as was his whole life."

"We should not even have come to his funeral."

"An informer is excluded from the Other World."

From the house, from the shadows of the death room, the wailing of Psalms hit against the panes of the window, and creaked as if they wanted to split the ears. From time to time cold jets of water swished and fizzled as the layers-out scrubbed down the stiff, hard body of the deceased, held in an upright position by the scouring board.

135

"They are washing him now," somebody remarked in the courtyard.

"If only his sins could be washed away so easily!" answered another voice.

"*And I will sprinkle clean water upon you, and ye shall be clean from all your uncleannesses . . . saith the Lord God*," was heard from the death chamber. For a few moments consternation swept across the courtyard. The jaunty comments suddenly fell silent, and the people, awed by the omnipotence of death, listened fearfully to the gloomy sounds that filtered through from the room in which the body-washers recited verses from the Song of Songs, as was their wont while engaging in their somber task.

"*His head is the most fine gold, his locks are curled and black as a raven.*"

"Now they are washing his head," someone remarked in a low voice.

"*His cheeks are as a bed of spices, as banks of sweet herbs; his lips are as lilies dropping with flowing myrrh.*"

The veil of piety was blown away for a moment, and again a few hard-mouthed comments could be heard:

"Well, from his lips no myrrh did ever flow, only hot oil with which he burned many people."

Inside again the swishing of jets of water could be heard, accompanied by a sad chant:

"*His hands are as rods of gold, set with beryl.*"

"Now they are washing his hands."

"It would be more proper to read for him from the Bible that 'the hands are the hands of Esau.'"

"Leave the poor fellow alone, he can no longer hurt anybody."

The desultory conversation was drowned out by the chant filtering through from the death chamber:

"*His legs are as pillars of marble, set upon sockets of fine gold.*"

"They are washing his legs now."

"*The roundings of thy thighs are like the links of a chain, the work of the hands of a skilled workman.*"

Out of the death chamber a whiff of fragrances wafted through the cracks of the window. Inside they were engaged in washing the body with spices.

"*Spikenard and saffron, calamus and cinnamon, with all trees of frankincense, myrrh, and aloes, with all the chief spices.*"

"You see," an old man suddenly spoke up in the crowd, "when we die we all become equal. They recite the Song of Songs for an informer just as they do for the most pious, most saintly Tzaddik."

"Death expiates everything."

Now the chant of robing could be heard from the death chamber:

"*I washed thee with water, yea, I cleansed away thy blood from thee, and I anointed thee with oil. I clothed thee also with richly woven work . . . and wound fine linen about thy head.*"

More and more people gathered. There was no longer room in the courtyard, and many of them had to remain outside, in the street, where they formed small groups.

"What a big funeral!"

"In his life everybody avoided him, and now everybody is here!"

"Only a funeral oration is needed to make it a really beautiful burial."

"What could be said about him? That he ruined many

people by informing against them? That this is how he made a living? There is no excuse for that. Not even death can expiate it."

The dead body, covered with a black sheet, was brought out of the death chamber, and put down in the courtyard. One more brief, silent prayer, then they took the coffin upon their shoulders, and the procession started.

Scarcely had they taken a few steps when a murmur of surprise ran through the crowd.

"The Rebbe is coming! The Rebbe is coming!"

"Can it be that he wants to give him the honor?"

"Is he possibly curious?"

"Or is he afraid not to come?"

The procession suddenly halted.

Silently they opened a way for the Tzaddik, who, clad in his floor-length black robe, with his head bent down sadly, approached the coffin. He wordlessly motioned the pallbearers to proceed. The procession moved silently, and only here and there could one hear the sad melody of the funereal Psalm: *"His truth is a shield and a buckler, thou shalt not be afraid of the terror by night."* Meanwhile the alms-collectors rattled their boxes: *"Charity saves from death."* But the donations dropped into the clanking boxes were few and far between. Everyone was occupied with the question of what could be in the mind of the great Tzaddik of Polonnoye, who was called the Great Chastiser, and would never say anything but the purest truth? But was it possible to tell the truth here? Would he not be arrested and thrown into jail? After all, the dead man was the hireling of the Castle! And, quite apart from that, was it permissible to shame the dead, any kind of dead?

The intelligence that the Tzaddik was present spread

quickly, and within a few minutes the funeral procession grew tenfold. The big and the little of the city hurried after him. All wanted to hear what the Great Chastiser had to say.

They left the outskirts of the city far behind. A heavy autumnal fog lay upon the fields and roads. The cemetery with its small stones became visible only when they stood directly in front of the gray "tent" of the dead.

The pallbearers put down the coffin. Everyone waited with baited breath, tensely. For a few moments the Tzaddik stood speechless in the gloomy, stressful silence, sunk into himself, and then began to speak in the slow, whining tone of funerary orations:

"There was once a dog. . . ."

The eyes suddenly flared up with a worrisome astonishment. The hearts of many were seized with fear. What if they should come to learn of it in the Castle?

The Tzaddik continued undisturbed:

"The name of the dog was Britan, and its master loved it because when he went hunting it caught the finest game. And one day the dog died."

"Did you see?" a woman whispered to her neighbor. "The Tzaddik pointed at the coffin."

"Be quiet. That is not possible."

The Tzaddik, raising his voice a little, continued:

"Among the animals there was a great rejoicing that they were rid of Britan, the big dog. But the fox, the most clever among the animals, rebuked them: 'Why should you be glad, you fools? Had he died before the other dogs learned from him how to catch game there would be place for rejoicing. But now that the others too have learned it, it will only be worse than hitherto. For until now, when the

other dogs saw that whatever they caught Britan snatched from their mouths and carried it to their master, who always fondled only Britan, they stopped catching, thinking, why should they exert themselves for somebody else. But now that this Britan died, now every dog will try hard to catch as much as he can so that he should become the master's pet. And in place of one dog there will be many dogs. Why, then, should you be glad?'"

Here the Tzaddik fell silent. He remained in his place excitedly, with flaring eyes, trembling in all his body. Then he suddenly raised his right hand high up, like a man who is about to threaten somebody. He hit the coffin three times with his palm, and cried:

"Bury the dead!"

The Tzaddik turned and hurried to the carriage that was waiting for him before the gate of the cemetery. Eyes that had become rigid with deep shock followed him. He quickly mounted the carriage together with his disciple, and drove home. A big shaggy black dog ran after the carriage. The soul of the informer must have entered into it, thought the believers.

All the way home the Tzaddik sat silently, sunk in deep thought. Then, hesitatingly, silently, he began to move his lips, as if he were speaking to an invisible, haunting soul. Finally he turned to his disciple.

"You too, my son," he addressed his disciple softly, "should say a prayer for the dead. You see, this soul, who strayed from the right path, would have had no chances at all to be saved. But by shaming the dead man I punished him, expiated the sins of his life, and thus saved a soul in Israel for the Heavenly Hall of Souls."

——15——

Story about the Story

or two years I sat at the feet of the world-famous Reb Shaye, who brought up his small pupils on the knees of the Torah. The happy parents, who sent their children to him from all corners of the world, knew well that two years with Reb Shaye were worth more than twelve with another master. I was not yet eleven when I went to him, and within a few weeks I knew many things that elsewhere were revealed only to adults, in fact, often only to those who had passed their fortieth year.

Reb Shaye was not stingy with giving either *kest* (food) or instruction, but especially the latter. We studied at dawn, we studied in the morning, we studied in the afternoon, we studied at night. For who knows at which moment is the Hour of Grace when one single sacred word weighs more than ten whole tractates at other times.

We also knew from the Talmud that "the breath of chil-

dren occupied with the Holy Writ maintains the world."
And who would not have gladly accepted the small sacrifice of constant study when the fate of the world depended
on each breath! We did not even get too tired of the cease-
less work, and when after studying for seven or eight hours
we went out into the fresh air and saw on the main street
of Kisvárda the big manor house supported by two huge
stone giants with enormous bulging muscles, we flexed
our thin arms and felt that we too were such giants who
supported the universe. And what is a manor house compared to the universe!

We knew also the Sabbath prayer, which had to be enun-
ciated with special care, for if one ran together in it two
separate sentences, the meaning that emerged was such
that it could destroy the whole world. And we certainly
were very careful about it. We knew that every word of a
prayer recited with true attention and devotion could help
an erring soul get to heaven, an erring soul that sinned in
its thoughts precisely at this word, and was condemned
to new wandering on earth. And we envied the adults, who
could pray with the *tefillin* on arm and head, and could
help in the achievement of eternal bliss and rest also by
those lost souls which were condemned to entering the
bodies of animals, and could obtain release only if out of
the skin of those animals straps were made for the *tefillin*,
and a pure soul prayed with them.

Only once were we caught up in a real *Weltschmerz*,
when Reb Shaye denied us the explanation of a kabbalistic
"secret," and we, with wounded self-esteem, decided in our
rebellious mood that we would put an end to everything.
On the Sabbath we gathered early in the synagogue and,
holding on to each other, with closed eyes, shaking and

trembling, we recited that fateful prayer, running the sentences together so that we were sure the synagogue would collapse upon us and go up in flames like Sodom. We came to only when the *shammash*, the synagogue's sexton, entered, and frightened us by shouting:

"What are you doing up there, you rascals!?"

We looked at each other with aching hearts. We knew nothing. We don't even know how to destroy the world.

We could barely be comforted. All day long we walked about with gloomy faces, and only toward evening, when to the accompaniment of beautiful songs we could enjoy the leftovers of the farewell meal of Queen Sabbath, did we cheer up a little.

In between the songs Reb Shaye would tell us wonderful stories. And we concluded from the stories that we were still too small, too weak. After all, what had we done up to that time except study? We had to wait for the time of deeds.

* * *

Every Sabbath evening Reb Shaye would tell us about the miraculous deeds of a Tzaddik, and we hung on his lips with rapt attention. He had an inexhaustible store of stories. After every song there came the turn of a story, and we regretted that the number of Sabbath evening songs was so small.

But once, as if the source had dried up, not a single story came to Reb Shaye's mind. We sang, with ardor and yearning, finished song after song, but Reb Shaye had no story to tell. We sadly intoned the last song, and our voices mourned over the wasted evening, the stories that were not born.

Suddenly Reb Shaye interrupted us:

"I have it, boys! It is a story about that Reb Avromele, who once could nowise think of any story."

And right away he started to tell it to us:

Before the Baal Shem died, he distributed everything he had among his disciples, and instructed his faithful attendant, Reb Avromele, to go from town to town and tell of those marvels of which he himself was an eyewitness. The telling of those stories would provide sufficient livelihood for Reb Avromele's large family. The Tzaddik died—peace be upon him!—and Reb Avromele followed his instruction faithfully. He traveled all over the world, and poured out the stories, and wherever he went he was received with love and respect, for everybody liked to hear about the miraculous deeds of the Baal Shem.

Once it happened that Reb Avromele learned that in Kosov there lived a rich old Jew, Reb Zishe by name, who was offering a gold piece for every story told him about the Baal Shem. So he, the master of stories, went there, and after a long and arduous journey arrived in the house of Reb Zishe, where he was received with great joy and jubilation. It was Friday afternoon, the house was filled with the spicy aroma of the Sabbath food, and Reb Zishe gave orders that they should prepare the finest dishes for the honored guest, who would season the meals of Queen Sabbath with the fragrance of stories about the Baal Shem.

The people of the house waited excitedly for the wonderful tales they expected to hear, and Reb Zishe himself looked forward with great expectation to enjoying the delectable moments. In the evening he seated his guest next to himself at the head of the table. After the blessing over the *Kiddush* cup and the breaking open of the Sabbath loaves, delicious gefilte fish was placed upon the white table, but most of those who sat around it had no patience to eat, and barely touched the fine food. Reb Zishe rushed through the first Sabbath song, and then, almost impatiently, said:

"And now, Reb Avromele, let us hear a story."

All ears pricked up, all eyes centered on Reb Avromele, who moved his head as if he were preparing to speak. But his lips remained silent. The silence became embarrassing. Reb Avromele rubbed his forehead with his hand, and then spoke sadly:

"Nothing comes to my mind at the moment. Perhaps after the soup."

The murmur of surprise could be heard all along the table. Annoyed, they spooned the hot soup. Then came the turn of another Sabbath song, after which they waited for the story.

Reb Avromele again tried to get underway, but to no avail.

"Perhaps after the meat," he said despondently.

The people sitting around the table began to think that the stranger was not at all the storyteller, but an impostor who was making a fool of them. Course after course was dished up and consumed, air after air was sung, but nothing, nothing would come to Reb Avromele's mind.

The host himself got up from the table chagrined, but Reb Avromele reassured him that by tomorrow he would certainly remember something; after all, he knew so many stories that all his life he had never run out of them.

But next day it was the same. The second, the third meal of the Sabbath came and went, and the story still did not appear. Evening fell. Reb Zishe made a last attempt, had the guest sit at the table to partake in the farewell meal of Queen Sabbath, but even then Reb Avromele could remember no story. Finally, greatly troubled, he decided that he would leave next morning.

Sunday morning he stood before the host, broken and ashamed, asked his forgiveness for having caused him such disappointment, said good-bye to him, and prepared to leave.

But just as he opened the door, he suddenly slapped his forehead, stopped, and turned back:

"At long last, there is something!"

Reb Zishe was filled with joy, and rushed up to Reb Avromele, who told him this story while they were standing right there at the door:

One Friday afternoon the Baal Shem issued orders that they should quickly harness the horses to his carriage, because he had to leave right away. I was surprised, and could not imagine where he would want to go so late, for within an hour the Sabbath would begin. But the Baal Shem cried, "Let's go!"

We quickly mounted the carriage, and the horses began to race, as if they were soaring in the air. The driver fell asleep, and the horses flew across forests, mountains, and waters. My whole body shook, but I did not dare ask where we were going. At last we entered a town, and in one of the streets we stopped and alighted. At that moment an old man leaned out of one of the windows, and called out to us in a fearful, tremulous voice:

"Run from here, run from this town, the people want to slaughter the Jews, the crowd is gathered in the main square, where the pope [priest of the orthodox church] is inciting them against the Jews."

The Baal Shem cast a piercing glance at the old man, and went on. I walked next to him without a word. Soon we reached the main square. A huge crowd was standing there, surrounding a platform on which a black-clad priest with bloodshot eyes held forth, haranguing the crowd, sawing the air with both arms. The people shouted:

"Death to the Jews! Let's go!"

The Baal Shem went on straight to the crowd, and when he reached it, the people turned around, surprised, and, as if they were frightened, opened a path for him. The Baal Shem mounted the platform and looked at the pope, whereupon the latter fell silent. The Baal Shem took hold of the pope's hand, and whispered something into his ear. The pope listened to him without making a move, as if he had turned into stone. Then, suddenly, he fell upon the Baal Shem's shoulders, and started to sob aloud.

The assembled crowd watched without understanding what was happening. Neither did I understand anything. The Baal Shem came down, joined me, and led me by my hand to the carriage. We mounted, and flew back the same way to Medzibozh. The whole community was already assembled in the synagogue, waiting for the Tzaddik. The Baal Shem went up to the Holy Ark, began to pray, and his face shone as the sun in the month of *Tammuz*. Never before had I seen it shine thus. After the prayer I went up to him to ask him where we had been and what had happened, but the Tzaddik stopped me before I could open my mouth:

"Don't ask anything. Time will come when you will understand."

Reb Avromele looked at his host, and saw that his face was all aglow, and tears flowed from his eyes like two silk threads.

"Reb Zishe! This is the end of the story. I don't know more about it."

Reb Zishe shook, grasped the hands of the storyteller, and it seemed as if in those few minutes his voice, his demeanor, his entire being had changed.

"I know the rest of the story, Reb Avromele. The pope, who at that time incited the people against the Jews, was converted by the appearance of the Baal Shem. From him he learned that his parents were Jews, from whom he was abducted in his childhood, and brought up to be a Jew hater. The pope quieted down the excited crowd, and distributed among them his extensive landed properties. He himself set out to wander, went from town to town, lived on bread and water, slept in the streets, was an unknown beggar. Thus he spent ten years of his atonement, then settled down here in Kosov, where nobody knew who he was, what he was. All the gold that he had acquired with his sins, that he had dragged along in his years of penance, he gave to his poor brethren. He did much good, and waited and waited that somebody would come and tell him his story. . . . For the Tzaddik had told me that if I should hear my story from somebody else, that will be the sign that my sins have been forgiven."

Of course, Reb Avromele did not leave the house of his host. He had his wife and children join him, and once they all were together he often retold the wonderful story, and each time tears of joy bathed the face of Reb Zishe.

The rest of the story was not known even to our master Reb Shaye. And we felt as if the soul of Reb Avromele had lived on in Reb Shaye, and we were the grandchildren of that Reb Zishe, and that is why we had to hear this story at the last minute, so that we should help the heavenly purification of our grandfather's soul.

—16—

The Etrog from the Holy Land

he Tzaddik of Rymanow was walking impatiently up and down in his room, and from time to time looked out the window, like someone awaiting an important guest.

"Go, my son, see whether Khezkele isn't coming yet," he said, turning to one of his young followers.

The young man considered it a great distinction to be given the task by the Tzaddik. He quickly ran out of the room, and a moment later returned:

"I don't see him yet. Shall I go to meet him?"

The Tzaddik nodded, then sat down for a moment. However, soon he again jumped up and hurried to the window.

"Where can that Khezkele tarry so long? Where can he be?"

Reb Sholem, the Torah scribe, asked timidly:

"Shall I go to see whether he is coming?"

The Tzaddik again indicated consent, but continued to look out the window.

"That Khezkele, that Khezkele, why is he so tardy? I cannot understand!"

Reb Khayeml, the second synagogue servant, offered also to go to meet Khezkele. Within less than a quarter of an hour some ten men went to meet the fervently awaited man. And the Tzaddik ran with increasing impatience from door to window and from window to door, repeating all the time:

"Where can he tarry? Where can he be?"

Suddenly, as he again reached the window, he stopped, and his eyes shone happily. All the believers thronged to the window, and saw that a group of men was approaching down the street. A minute later Khezkele, together with a sizable company, entered the room. The Tzaddik ran to meet him at the door, and snatched from his hand the small package, which, after having crossed stormy seas and passed through many countries, had finally arrived by the Rymanow mail. The Tzaddik quickly pried open the thin, longish wooden box, and one by one removed its precious contents and placed them on the table. First he unrolled a slender, green palm frond, then took out a few fragrant myrtle branches, and finally, out of a special little box, he removed the lemon-shaped *etrog*. He put everything side by side on the table, and looked at it for a long while silently, touched with emotion.

"You see, my children, this palm frond, which is like the spine of a man, this myrtle whose leaves are like a man's eyes, and this *etrog* which is like a human heart, they all come from the Holy Land from which all blessing spreads upon the world. The tree of the *etrog*, the trunk of the palm

tree, and the bush of the myrtle are all still there. Their roots are anchored in the depth of the soil and imbibe the sacred moisture that trickles down from the eternal rivers of the Garden of Eden. You see, my friends, the fruit of the *etrog* was cut off from its tree, the palm frond from its trunk, but the roots have remained in the blessed soil. And when the Children of Israel pray with the *etrog* and *lulav* in their hands, and out of their mouths, which are like the leaves of the weeping willow surrounding the festive palm frond, a yearning supplication gushes forth toward heaven —the branches of the World Tree up there in the Heights begin to hum, the Bird's Nest trembles, the chirpings fall silent, a deep sigh fills the Universe, and the Ancient of Days is filled with mercy for His exiled children."

The Tzaddik again took the *etrog* in his hands, and stroked it, stroked it lovingly. And as he passed his thin sensitive fingers over the knobs of the fruit, he felt as if his soul were wandering on the grassy downs of the Sharon, among the sacred trees whose fruits had been torn away and scattered in so many far lands.

A loud, piercing cry awakened the Tzaddik from his reverie. Reb Rakhmilke, the Tzaddik's famous decorator of Sukkot booths, burst into the room:

"Rebbe! The booth is finished. It is ready for the Rebbe to see!"

"I am coming, my son," said the Tzaddik gently.

The curious guests pushed forward to see the wonders wrought by Reb Rakhmilke. And while they admired the many ornaments adorning the walls—the colored stars, the Magen Davids, the lions carved in wood, the lampions and gilded fruits hanging from the roof of green branches—they began to discuss the *etrog* of the Tzaddik.

"Isn't the. *etrog* beautiful?" asked Reb Sholem of his neighbor.

"Of course, of course," answered Reb Khone, but he did not add anything to the praise, as was his wont.

Reb Khezkl was more courageous and did not hesitate to be outspoken:

"My *etrog* is more beautiful. Much more beautiful."

"Mine too. The Rebbe's *etrog* does not even end in a cone, as it is prescribed!"

"After all, the *etrogs* of Corfu are more beautiful."

"Not only more beautiful, but also better. They conform better to the prescription."

"Did you notice that the Rebbe's *etrog* has a gray spot near its tip? The Rebbe failed to notice it, but my sharp eyes did not miss it."

"And the knobs and dents are not as they should be."

"In Lublin it is not even allowed to use *etrogs* from the Holy Land. The Tzaddik of Lublin himself prohibited it."

"And the *lulav*, did you like it?"

"It is a little crooked."

"Nor are the myrtle leaves equidistant from one another."

"Silence! The Rebbe is coming!"

The animated conversation ceased at once. The Tzaddik appeared in the doorway. In his hands he held the *lulav* and the *etrog* from the Holy Land, and his face shone happily. The believers looked at him with awe and reverence.

But as the Tzaddik was about to step across the threshold of the booth, his foot was caught and he stumbled. His hand shook, and the *etrog* fell to the floor.

A great fright swept through those assembled in the booth. All of them looked at the ground, to see whether the *etrog* suffered any damage.

"Its tip broke off! It is finished!" went the sad news from mouth to mouth.

"The *pitem* broke off! Woe! The *pitem* broke off!"

The shiver of the fateful accident ran through all those who were there in the booth, and no longer did each of them think of the glory that his *etrog* was more beautiful than that of the Tzaddik. They all looked with pity at the Tzaddik and at his *etrog*. All of them knew that it was too late to obtain a new *etrog*, and as it was, the damaged *etrog* could not be used. The reason that the *etrog* was always wrapped in soft hemp was precisely to protect it, to prevent the tip from breaking off. And now the *pitem* had broken off! What a misfortune!

The Tzaddik looked sadly at the damaged fruit of the Holy Land, and two big drops of tear ran down his furrowy cheeks.

"Let me give my *etrog* to the Rebbe," said Reb Sholem compassionately.

"Mine is more beautiful," interrupted Reb Khezkl. "Let the Rebbe take mine!"

The Tzaddik looked around, and asked in a sorrowful voice:

"Are your *etrogs* from the Holy Land?"

The people kept silent. Then from the back a voice could be heard:

"The *etrogs* of Corfu are more beautiful."

The Tzaddik did not answer. He took the damaged fruit of the Holy Land, wiped off the dust that was clinging to it, and gently tied it around with the pure flax as one bandages the bleeding wounds suffered by a beloved friend.

"What will the Rebbe do?" asked Reb Khezkl.

"I shall use my *etrog*," answered the Tzaddik. "The small-

est piece of fruit from the Holy Land is worth more than the most perfect fruit brought from the strange lands that are subjugating Israel. The *etrog* has been damaged, but its roots are there in the blessed land. And when the Children of Israel leave their houses, enter the booths, and recognize that they have no safe haven anywhere except in the booth of God's protection, when they press the *etrog* to their hearts, direct their eyes to the myrtle, and raise the palm frond toward heaven, then across all the distances the fruit reunites with its tree, the branch grows together with the trunk, and the Ancient of Days becomes filled with compassion for His exiled children."

The guests of the booth looked at one another with surprise. And the Tzaddik carefully placed the damaged *etrog* from the Holy Land in its sparkling glass case, and began to view with pleasure the marvelous decorations of the booth prepared by Reb Rakhmilke in honor of the feast.

—17—

The Twelve Sabbath Breads

I

he evening enveloped the streets of Safed, and all around the hills caught a glow, like festive farewell fires lighting up the way of the departing Queen Sabbath. In the House of Study, in the mysterious semidarkness, around the long cloth-covered table, the disciples of Luria sat shoulder to shoulder and listened with rapt attention to the low voice of the Master. The Third Meal of the Sabbath was nearing its end. The remaining small pieces of the white Sabbath bread sat modestly, barely visibly, amid the folds of the white table-cloth, waiting for the holy prayer, to receive the last blessing. Luria rested his elbows on the table, and with his head bent low spoke almost inaudibly.

"The children of the royal palace know when the time of the royal repast arrives. They put on their cambric

robes, and dressed in pure white go to receive the King
and the Queen. He who does not go to the repast is not
from among the children of the palace. And at the Third
Meal of the Sabbath, when the Queen takes leave of her
children, the Time of Mercy arrives, shining gates open
all around, and a thousand sparkling lights flare up
through a thousand doors. And a voice can be heard from
inside: 'Come, my holy people, come, my dear children,
go with jubilation to receive your Lord, with jubilant
happiness and complete joy, for the Time of Mercy is
here!'"

The Master fell silent. With his finger he pointed at one
of his disciples who sat to the side. The youth understood
the sign, and in a soft, wistful voice intoned the song of
the Third Meal:

> The sons of the palace desire
> To see the face of their Holy Sire.

The whole House of Study was filled with the sounds
of the song. Snatches of the melody wheeled about between the graying walls like white butterflies in the dark-
ening dusk of the evening. Through the windows the last
shimmer of light sneaked into the room to mingle with
the mysterious, sweet melodies. Luria listened to the song
without a word, sunk into himself, and then continued,
while darkness increasingly covered his face:

"And when the Children of Israel gather for the meals
of Queen Sabbath, and sing holy songs over the twelve
breads, each of whose braids is like double the holy letter
of the Lord's Name, the voice of Judgment becomes the
voice of Compassion, the Mercy of Mercies arrives, and

the Ancient of Days is filled with joy, as he was in the days of old, when the twelve breads were lying on the altar of the Sanctuary, so that blessing, bread, and well-being should pour forth from it to the whole world. This is the mystery of the twelve breads. And this is the Sabbath meal of the Holy King, from which plenty, joy, and happiness flow onto all the days of the week."

The Master again sank into thought. The disciple intoned a new Sabbath song. Those who sat around him accompanied his singing with a low, humming rhythm:

> Shining majesty, light of the world,
> My soul is sick with Your love,
> O God, heal it with Your radiance,
> Cast on it Your glorious glance.

Outside it was fully dark now. The shining eyes of the stars sent sweet glances through the windows of the House of Study. And those who looked out, and those who looked in, could see that the King was soaring on his resplendent throne-chariot across the infinite, and next to him sat Sabbath, the Queen, with a sparkling crown on her head, and from the precious stones of her diadems light radiated upon the entire world.

Suddenly the room was lighted up. The sexton brought in two burning candles, and put them down on the middle of the table. The wonderful visions disappeared in a moment. It was as if the Sabbath soul had flown out of every body, to give her place to the wingless, gray spirit of the weekdays.

The Master lifted up the silver cup of wine, and in sadness monotonously intoned the aftermeal prayer.

II

Avigdor, the old Safed tailor, silently left the House of Study just before the two candles lighted up the faces of the assembled. He had slipped into Luria's House of Study under cover of the gathering dusk, sat down modestly in a dark corner, and listened in a daze to the words of the Master and the mysterious songs of the disciples. Only a few words, those that were simple and clear, managed to penetrate his mind. But even those few words were sufficient to perturb him, and to drive restlessness into his heart. He felt that his life had been so small, so empty, that it had run its course in small stitches of the needle. He would have liked to take part in that life that created worlds and saw new worlds everywhere. And as he was sauntering homeward in the dark, silent streets, the holy words and the sacred songs continued to ring in his ears, and suddenly he was seized with the feeling that his soul too had acquired wings with which he, the poor tailor, could also fly up into the infinite heights. He quickened his steps so as to tell his helpmeet the wonderful discovery.

"Leah, I want to tell you wonderful secrets. I sat in the House of Study with Luria at the Third Meal of the Sabbath, and heard words of the holy Kabbalah."

"What could you have heard?" asked Leah with curiosity.

Old Avigdor tried to gather his thoughts. But in vain did he knit his brows into a thousand wrinkles. He could not remember anything.

"Out there in the dark I knew all the time what I would tell you. But here, in the light of the oil lamp, I've forgotten everything."

"Shall I put out the lamp?"

"No, no, Granny," protested old Avigdor. "In fact, I do remember. The Master spoke of the twelve Sabbath breads that were placed on the altar of the ancient Sanctuary."

"And what did he say about them?"

"He said that from them did spread plenty, blessing, and bread into the whole world."

"So that's why now there is no blessing and no bread, because the Temple of Jerusalem was destroyed," sighed Leah.

"Of course," said Avigdor, satisfied that his helpmeet got right what he was thinking. "For that very reason I have a very big idea. To you I shall reveal it."

"Tell me quickly!" said Leah impatiently.

"I want to help the misery of the world."

"How?" asked Leah surprised.

"Very simply," answered Avigdor quietly. "But you too have to help me, Leah."

Leah looked at him questioningly. And Avigdor continued with pride:

"You will bake, Granny, twelve Sabbath breads every Friday, each with twelve braids, and I shall put them into the Holy Ark before dark, when as yet there is nobody in the synagogue. Let there be again plenty, bread, blessing, and happiness in the world, as there was in the days of the Temple of Jerusalem."

Leah happily nodded her assent. Her frail, bent husband grew tall in her eyes, almost like the High Priest of Jerusalem. After all, he too would present an offering on the altar of God for the whole world.

And Friday afternoon old Avigdor was the first to arrive in the synagogue. He looked around timidly, and sneaked in with the twelve small breads hidden under his coat. His whole body trembled as he walked up the steps to the Holy Ark. He hastily pulled aside the sacred curtain, opened the door, and quickly hid the breads behind the Torah scrolls, while he murmured, trembling feverishly, the short prayer he himself had composed: "Lord of the Universe! Accept the offering of Your small servant, and send plenty and blessing to the world, Amen!"

III

Barely did the dawn of the Sabbath rise when Reb Hayyim, the faithful servant of the synagogue, set out to open the House of Prayer, change the curtain of the Holy Ark, and place new mantles on the Torah scrolls and a new cover on the lectern. He clad all of them in white, so that they should receive in white purity the sacred Sabbath of Remembrance. From the drawers of the lectern he took out the white, silver-embroidered mantles, hurried up to the Ark, and quickly opened it. The small bells attached to the Torah mantles tinkled jubilantly, as if they were greeting the holy scrolls lined up side by side. Reb Hayyim lifted out one of them, to put the white festive mantle on it. Suddenly he started. He could not believe his eyes. Behind the scrolls there were twelve little Sabbath breads lying in a row.

"The Torah has been desecrated! Sacrilege!" he cried, and fury gleamed in his eyes.

For quite a while he tried to figure it out, but in vain. Who could have done it? No Jew would sink to doing such a thing. Perhaps some Muslim unbeliever wanted to make a mockery of the Children of Israel, by showing that they were but idol worshipers.

And Reb Hayyim made up his mind that he would get to the bottom of the thing. Day and night he prowled about the synagogue, trying to espy the mysterious stranger. Friday afternoon, as he was standing behind the synagogue, he saw a small, bent figure approach. He had no difficulty in recognizing old Avigdor.

"What could the old tailor want so early in the synagogue?" wondered Reb Hayyim.

The wizened old man hugged his big, long coat tightly about him as he sneaked into the synagogue. Reb Hayyim silently followed him to the door, and watched. The steps of the old tailor grew fainter as he approached the Holy Ark. Reb Hayyim peeped curiously through the keyhole, and almost dropped in astonishment.

Old Avigdor was standing there before the open Ark. His face shone with happiness when he saw that the old Sabbath breads were no longer there. God had accepted his offering. One by one he took out the new breads from under his coat, and put them carefully into the Ark. And with eyes closed he recited his prayer.

Reb Hayyim could stand it no longer. He tore open the door, and rushed in, shouting furiously:

"You miserable fellow! You pagan! What are you doing!?"

Old Avigdor shook with fright. His whole body became petrified. He did not even turn around, but collapsed, and fell unconscious among the sacred scrolls.

A great fear gripped Reb Hayyim's heart.

"Avigdor! Avigdor!" he cried. "Get up! What did you do!?"

But old Avigdor lay there before the Holy Ark, with glazed-over eyes, his hands clutching at one of the sacred scrolls.

"Almighty Lord! He is dead!" cried Reb Hayyim, and ran deranged out of the synagogue.

IV

The people quickly gathered in the synagogue. Some were brought early by their piety, others by the terrible news. In the courtyard they discussed the event somberly.

"It was the punishment of God," said Reb Hayyim. "Let us only hope that no blow will be visited on us as well."

"The sons of Aaron the High Priest also died in the Sanctuary, because they brought an offering that was not commanded," added one of the others.

"But how could such a thing come to poor Avigdor's mind?" wondered another.

"Perhaps the soul of an ancient sinful sacrificer was living in him," said one of Luria's disciples.

In the meantime Luria himself arrived, clad in a floor-length white Sabbath robe. One of the disciples motioned the crowd aside, and they quickly opened a path for the Master.

Luria stepped straight up to the dead man, looked at him with tearful eyes, and said with a voice trembling with pain:

"We must mourn and bewail this dear deceased right here inside the synagogue, as we do a saint who sacrifices his life to the Lord. God, who can see into all hearts, searches only the heart, and I can verily tell you that ever since Aaron the High Priest there has been nobody who so delighted the Lord of the Universe with his heartfelt offering as this happy dead Tzaddik. In the sacred flame of his act his soul rose so high from his body that a single word was able to liberate it completely. Happy is he whose heart is so immaculate, happy he whose intention is so immaculate. He did not know the secrets of the Torah, but his soul was pure, and it is flying up in purity on the wings of the Shekhinah into the Hall of Souls, where the Ancient of Days is receiving with smiles His late holy sacrificer."

—18—

Velvele of Zbarazh

 hat the Zbarazher Reb Velvele was a world-shaking Tzaddik, that with his prayer he could perform miracles in the Above and the Below, that with his Torah he could uproot mountains and crumble them into powder—all this was well known to every child, not only in Zbarazh, but in the whole world. Only Reb Velvele himself knew nothing of it. He simply sat and studied, or stood and prayed, or walked and cogitated. But what the people wanted of him—that he did not understand. They came to him from everywhere, asking for Torah, prayer, advice. But Reb Velvele would answer astonished:

"The Children of Israel are all saints, and all are dear to the Lord of the World."

Pilgrims would come to him to spend with him a Sabbath, a Holy Day. And Reb Velvele was surprised: why should they come to him from so far, when the Sabbath and the Holy Days of the Lord were sacred everywhere, and their observance pleasing to the Almighty? But, after all, one must make room for the guests at one's table, and one cannot send them back at such a late hour. In the eyes of Reb Velvele every man was saintly, whether he was one of his followers or not, and even when speaking to his coachman he would say:

"My saint, why do you hurt those poor horses, when they trot fast enough?"

When two quarreling men came to him, and each of them presented his case with much excitement and flailing of arms, Reb Velvele would answer humbly:

"How could I decide between two such saintly men? It will be best if you make peace, my brothers."

Once he saw that his wife was arguing with her maid, because the girl hired herself out to a better-paying house without giving her due notice.

"I shall not let you go!" the *rebbetzin* cried angrily.

"I shall not stay! Let's go to the judge!" the maid answered back defiantly.

Reb Velvele saw that his wife was putting on her coat, whereupon he too put on his festive robe and fur cap, and made ready to go with her.

"Where are you going?" the woman asked, puzzled.

"To the law court, my dear!" answered the Tzaddik modestly.

"It does not behoove you to go to such a place. Nor is it necessary, since I am quite capable of protecting my interests."

"Yes," the Tzaddik answered mildly, "but is the poor maid capable of protecting her interest?"

"Don't tell me that you want to protect her?" said the woman, taken aback.

"Why not, my sweet saint? There is no shame in that. Is it not written in the Book of Job, 'Did I despise the cause of my man-servant or of my maid-servant'?"

The weather was stormy and freezy when the poor shop-keeper of the neighboring village invited the Tzaddik to participate in the nocturnal vigil after the birth of his son. Reb Velvele accepted the sacred duty gladly. Next day the child would be eight days old, and at that time, especially about midnight, a host of evil spirits lurks around the cradle, trying to snatch away the innocent soul before the child is introduced next day into the sacred Covenant of Abraham.

It was late in the evening when the Tzaddik's rickety cart started out on its way. The road was covered with heavy snow, and the horses had difficulty on the slippery surface, so that it was almost midnight by the time Reb Velvele arrived in the village. He asked the driver to come in with him into the house, but the man wanted to stay outside to watch over the cart and the horses, lest somebody make off with them.

Inside, in the room hung all about with angelic names and protective tablets, the assembled guests greeted the Tzaddik with jubilant joy. Reb Velvele sat with them for about half an hour, and then got up and went out. The people thought he would return in a minute or so, and nobody followed him outside. But time passed, they waited, waited, a quarter of an hour, half an hour, an hour, and the Tzaddik still did not return. The host and the guests became impatient, and the hearts of many were filled with worry. After all, it was past midnight, in the house there was an eight-day-old child, who knows what happened out there? Perhaps the Tzaddik was struggling with evil spirits, and who knows who will prevail?

Finally, the whole group of guests timidly ventured out into the courtyard. Outside it was dark and stormy, only the snow, stirred up by the wind, gave off some light. The little group did not dare to break up, to set out to search separately, but stayed together, and sheltering in each others' bodies they slid down the white snow like a big dark skein. Suddenly, as they got to the gate, they saw the Tzaddik walking up and down before the horses and the cart, sunk deep in thought, his moustache, his sidelocks, his beard all covered with icicles.

"What is the Rebbe doing here?" the devotees asked astonished, and one of them hurried up to him and quickly wrapped his big warm woolen shawl around the Tzaddik's shoulders.

Reb Velvele answered quietly, as if nothing had happened:

"I came out to enable the coachman to go in to the kitchen for a while, to get warm. I told him I would watch over the horses in the meantime. And he has not yet returned."

When the followers returned into the house they found the Tzaddik's coachman in the kitchen, next to the oven, wrapped in his furry cloak, and sound asleep.

"Reb Velvele has no match!" said the believers admiringly.

But Reb Velvele believed with all his heart that he was in no way better than the other Children of Israel. After all, in Israel even a sinner sins only because he is ignorant

of the source of his soul. When culpable souls came to him
so that he impose a penance upon them, he said, "If you
want to do penance, you are saintly and don't have to
undertake a special penance." There was only one thing
he could not understand: how was it possible that there
were people to whom God gave much riches, and who still
did not give a share of it to others, to those in need? But
he found an excuse even for them: the poor ignorant souls
did not know why the Lord of the World gave them all
that treasure.

When Reb Velvele heard that a rich innkeeper in
Zbarazh never gave alms to the poor, he went to him, sat
down next to him on the bench of the tavern, and gently
started to tell him a story:

"Once upon a time there lived in a city two brothers.
One was poor, the other very rich. The rich brother was
beneficent, he loved his brother, and supported him with
everything. When his brother fell on bad days, he lent him
a thousand florins to enable him to find a new livelihood.
Then the wheel of fortune turned. The poor brother became richer and richer, and the rich one became ruined.
But the newly rich brother was ungrateful, and did not
want to help his brother. He even refused to return the
thousand florins to his brother, who perished in great
misery. In heaven a harsh sentence was pronounced on
the hard-hearted brother, and soon thereafter he too died.
But the brother who was rich and became poor implored
heaven to have mercy on his brother, and offered to take
his punishment upon himself. 'I have long ago forgiven
him the thousand florins,' he said. The heavenly court of
justice decided that in any case he had to repay him the
thousand florins. Therefore both of them would have to

be born again: the brother who had become ruined would be born rich again, and his brother would have to work for him as a servant until he worked off his debt. 'Let rather my brother be born rich,' begged the goodhearted brother, 'and let me as a beggar receive back from him the thousand florins in the form of penny alms.' The heavenly court agreed, and the two brothers were born again on earth, one rich, one poor. But what happens if the rich brother, not knowing the source of his soul, does not pay off his old debt with alms?"

This is the story Reb Velvele told, and the avaricious tavern keeper became generous from that moment on, and distributed many times a thousand florins among the poor and the needy.

Reb Velvele never shamed anybody, and he had no opponents at all, in contrast to other Tzaddiks. When the faraway "great mountains" clashed, causing noise, confusion, and upheaval in the world, Reb Velvele was never among them. He quietly sat and studied, or stood and prayed, or walked and cogitated. And when one of his disciples once, out of curiosity, went to Lublin to spend a Holy Day there, the Tzaddik of Lublin said to him reproachfully:

"Go back to Zbarazh. From Zbarazh one does not have to go anywhere. With your Tzaddik even the weekday is a Holy Day. Reb Velvele has only one sin: he lies when in the prayer he utters the words of repentance: 'I have sinned.'"

—19—

The Tzaddik Count

 orty-two candles were burning at the head of the table and shed their light onto the flaming face of the great Tzaddik of Zanz, onto his great shining eyes, and onto his long, snow-white beard that fell down upon the white tablecloth. The believers who were sitting around the table sought with love and respect to glimpse the Tzaddik, whom the forty-two tall candlesticks, lined up in front of him like a guard of honor, shielded from the curious eyes. Those who sat farther off could see only a dazzling radiance, and, from time to time, the holy glint of eyes. Taken aback, they would lower their heads over the table, and listen to the Friday evening chant that poured out from behind the candles:

> Peace be unto you, angels of the Highest,
> Angels of peace, angels of heavens,

Blessed be the King of the Kings of Kings,
The Holy One, who sent you.

And when the Tzaddik rose, and with the brimful cup
in his hand sanctified the Sabbath, everyone saw the angels of peace flutter over his head and crown him with that
flowery wreath of "seventy over fifty."

Next to the wines of Carmel fine dishes came on the
table, and already at the welcoming of the sacred day the
Sabbath fish was steaming behind the candlesticks, spiced
with that magic spice whose name is Sabbath and whose
fragrance only those can feel into whom the Sabbath soul
enters on Friday night to maintain them in the festive mood
until the following evening, when Queen Sabbath bids
them farewell.

The Tzaddik of Zanz lifted up the cover from the fish
tureen, tasted the Sabbath dish, and, as if speaking to himself, said:

"Oh, if only I too could once taste that taste in the Sabbath fish, which the saintly Tzaddik Count Potoczki
felt."

"The Rebbe loves the fish?" a voice asked timidly.

The Tzaddik looked up nervously:

"Foolishness! Do I love the fish? To love food? Can the
fish love me? I love the Creator of the Universe!"

He ate a few pieces, and then shook his head sadly:

"Oh, if only I too could once work out the body as did
the saintly Tzaddik Count Potoczki."

Some of the followers, already acquainted with the sad
story of Count Potoczki who had converted to the Jewish
faith, understood the words of the Tzaddik. The others
listened with surprise.

* * *

Few are those who know to what high degree did rise not only his soul, but also his body! How it was cleansed of all earthly dross; how he soared, soared to such heights that not even the angels of heaven could follow him.

The angels were born in the heavens, no sin tempts them, neither passion, nor joy, nor anger. But he was born down here, in the Land of Israel's oppressors, a man of flesh and blood. He was brought up in purple and silk, and was rocked on the knees of the sins of his fathers' house.

And the child grew to be a youth, and the youth left the purple and silk, the castle and the garden, and went among the rags, among the thorns, into the backstreets of the poor, to seek the truth. And on his way he found the God of Israel and His Holy Torah.

The young count wandered, from Vilna to Rome, from Rome to Amsterdam, and, entering the Covenant of Abraham, his name became Abraham. And he ate bread with salt, and drank water with measure, and the bread for which he hungered became the Teaching, and the water for which he thirsted became the Torah.

And his mother came to him with her face covered by a veil, with a mourning countenance, and begged him, implored him:

"Come back to us, my son, return to the house of your father, and wipe away the great shame from us. Your splendid castle with its flower garden is waiting for you, and you live here in a shack, among strangers. Silk and purple are awaiting you at home, and you walk, clad in rags, among beggars. Rich repasts wait in sparkling halls, and you are starving here. Or is it that you believe in the Other World of these fools?"

And Rabbi Abraham Potoczki looked at his mother gently, and said:

"You think, O mother, that the hope of a reward in the Other World enticed me to come here to my new brethren. I swear to you, that even if I should know that my soul would never have a share in the heavenly salvation, even then I would stay here, and I would be satisfied with the earthly reward, the earthly pleasure of having recognized the truth. And believe me, O my mother, that if in the morning I can put on the silver-wreathed tallit, I have a greater joy than have our great lords when they dress in their silk and purple robes. And if in the evenings I can go to the House of Study, to delve into the truths of the Torah together with my brethren, my pleasure is greater than ever it was at home when we went to false theatrical plays, to vain entertainments. And if on Friday evenings, enriched with the Sabbath soul, I can taste the fish prepared for the Queen Sabbath, it is more enjoyable for me than all the fine dishes of the luxurious banquets that used to tickle my palate at home. Not for the World to Come am I here, but only for the earthly world, whose pleasures you too could find if you would stay with me, O my mother."

And Rabbi Abraham Potoczki broke down and wept, and grasped his mother's hands and covered them with his tears. But the countess proudly tore her hands out of her son's hands, and ran out of the room.

And Rabbi Abraham Potoczki delved into the mysteries of the Torah, deeper and deeper. And the time came for him to die a holy martyr's death for his new faith. His heart became filled with yearning for his mother, and he set out to visit the city of his birth, Vilna, to be able to see her in secret.

But his parents recognized him, and had him arrested.

He was thrown in jail, threatened, then tortured, and when he remained steadfast in his faith he was condemned to die on the stake.

And when the holy Tzaddik was taken out to the marketplace of Vilna to be burnt, and all the people of the city stood around the stake, he asked the permission of his judges to address his new brethren:

"Believe not that what you do is justice. Justice is with God, and I shall die trusting in Him. But let me say a few words to the sons of my faith."

And Rabbi Abraham Potoczki turned to the Jews, who were crying bitterly, and spoke to them, saying:

"Do not cry, do not wail for me, my brothers. All my life I was troubled by the thought that perhaps the body will not have its cleansing. From my soul the Torah burnt away all the slag, my soul was cleansed by the divine Teaching and the divine Service, but what would happen to the body that came from such a place? How would it rise up and be cleansed of the dross? And behold, God took pity on me, and now I can rejoice for my body too will be cleansed in the fire, and, behold, I can fly up like an angel of heaven to the heavenly Seat of Judgment, under the protecting wings of the Shekhinah."

And the holy Tzaddik threw himself into the flames, and cried at the top of his voice:

"Hear, O Israel, the Lord our God, the Lord is One!"

* * *

When the Tzaddik of Zanz concluded the story, tears shone in his eyes, and also the eyes of the followers, who sat around the table, were full of tears.

"Behold and know, how high can an elect of God rise. O height of heights! If only I too could work out the body as did the holy Tzaddik Count Potoczki."

Then he turned to his son who sat next to him:

"Continue the Sabbath song, my son."

And all around the table the Sabbath song resounded again:

> Hail to you, angels of God
> Angels of Peace, angels of heaven,
> Sent by the King of the Kings of Kings,
> The Holy One, blessed be He.

—20—

The Sons of Haman

ach time the New Moon of the month of Adar arrived, the face of the Tzaddik of Dynov was as if it had been transformed. The wrinkles of his brows smoothed, gone was the gloomy veil from his eyes (of which the initiated knew that it was that veil that saved the adherents from being singed by the fire of his glance), from his lips disappeared the bitter smile, which so many tried to explain but nobody really understood. His whole countenance shone with a happy serenity that slowly intensified into joy, jubilation, rapture.

The Tzaddik let his eyes rest with an indescribable pleasure on the walls, which at this time of the year his adherents covered with pictures, one more beautiful than the other. Not, of course, with sundry unholy paintings, but with splendid scenes depicting the story of Purim. King Ahasuerus celebrates his marriage with Esther. Haman forces the king to sign the decree about the extermination of the Jews. Esther and the mourning Mordecai meet. Esther before King Ahasuerus, the fasting Jews, the king at the feast given by Esther, the humiliation of Haman, the gallows, the triumph of Mordecai, the Jews celebrating Purim. And the Tzaddik becomes lost in reveries before this picture and that. My God, what miracles, what miracles, and still, how many times they were repeated, how many times!

And the figures, as the Tzaddik muses over them, slowly lose their features, the individuals become elevated to symbols. In place of Haman there stands before him the entire Jew-hating world. Instead of Mordecai, the persecuted Israel. Esther becomes the Shekhinah who protects her children. For a moment the face of the Tzaddik darkens, but then his glance is caught by the big letters over the door, which fill out the grey section of the wall left unpainted in memory of the destroyed Jerusalem, and which proclaim the message of glad tidings: "When Adar arrives one multiplies the joy!"

And the Tzaddik of Dynov multiplies the joy, with all his heart, with all his soul. The nearer the feast of Purim comes the more he is overpowered by intoxication. A few days prior to the holiday, but especially on the day of the Fast of Esther, he can no longer control himself, walks excited up and down his room, claps his hands, breaks into jubilation, and sings all kinds of songs, melodies which the peasants sing in the streets, airs with which they make merry in the tavern, but of course the Tzaddik sings them to Hebrew words.

And in the evening, when they went to the reading of the *Megillah*, the Tzaddik too bought for himself a little rattle in the synagogue courtyard, and each time the name of Haman was read, he joined in the noise-making of the children, whom it was almost impossible to quiet down on those occasions. He never read the *Megillah* himself, as was the custom of the other Tzaddiks, because his excitement was so intense that it was to be feared that in the course of reading the overwhelming joy could make his soul leave his body.

Next day, when he sat down with his followers to partake in the festive meal, he was totally inebriated even though not a drop of wine had passed his lips. It happened once, that one of the Hasidim surreptitiously emptied the cup of the Tzaddik each time, and the Tzaddik nevertheless became as intoxicated as if he himself had drunk all that wine.

Then came the time for the Purim jests. The masqueraders came, and the Tzaddik attentively watched their antics, encouraging them from time to time with an enthusiastic whoop.

About midnight they all looked curiously forward to the greatest of all Purim jests, which the Tzaddik himself was wont to improvise. The year before he took off his white silken caftan and gave it to the *gabbai* who accompanied him:

"Put it on, and do everything in my place!"

But luckily that substitution did not last long, because the *gabbai*, who was unprepared for the great power he suddenly received, almost turned upside down the whole order of the world.

What will the Tzaddik do this time?

As the clock struck twelve, the Tzaddik said:

"We go to Russka!"

The Hasidim looked at one another, frightened:

"To Russka? Among the sons of Haman?"

"In Russka, if the Russians see a Jew they beat him to death!"

"Last year poor Reb Hershele went near their boundary, and they stoned him!"

"To Russka! At midnight! And on a Sunday!"

"When all of them are carousing together in the tavern!"

"The rowdies will tear us to pieces!"

"It is rumored that they are planning to raid Dynov at Easter time and kill the Jews!"

The Tzaddik repeated quietly:

"We are going to Russka!"

Who would dare to disobey if the Tzaddik of Dynov commands something twice, and especially on the night of Purim?

The *gabbai* carried out his task. Soon the carriages were ready in the courtyard, and the procession got moving. In the first carriage sat the Tzaddik, and next to him the violinist Reb Hayyem, who, together with his three companions, played Russian peasant melodies all the way. The Tzaddik accompanied them with song, and the whole procession sang with him. And those who were graced with the ability to see visions noticed that the moon emerged from behind the clouds, and that in the moon sat King David and played his violin, and he played the same airs which they down here sang in the carriages.

At three o'clock great surprises took place in the tavern of Russka.

The door opened, and, to the great astonishment of the carousing peasants, there entered a hoary old man, clad in a white silk caftan. On his long white beard it seemed as if drops of wine were glittering, and his whole counte-

nance was aflame with rapture. Behind him followed four
Jewish musicians, stepping timidly into the big hall dense
with liquor fumes, and so full of reveling peasants that not
a single additional person seemed able to squeeze into it.
The others remained outside, and watched what was happening through the open door.

The peasants looked at each other, astonished. They
were so surprised that they could not utter a word. Silently
they made room for the strange visitors. The Tzaddik called
upon Reb Hershele the musician:

"Play!"

And even before the musicians could start to play, the
Tzaddik himself intoned the famous forbidden song:

> Sick is the poor little father,
> Bombs and guns will cheer him up.

The peasants huddled together.

"Spies!" whispered one of them. "Masked spies!"

"We better be careful!" went from mouth to mouth.
"Careful!"

The Tzaddik concluded the feared song, and then
turned to the peasants:

"Don't you know how to be merry? Don't you have
musicians? Hey, Vassily, innkeeper! Wine to everybody!
Here is the money!"

The glasses were filled with wine. The peasants, used to
the burning brandy, reached timidly, hesitatingly, for the
expensive, luxurious drink. A few of them nevertheless took
a chance, tossed up a glass, and the others followed their
example. Reb Hayyem and his band intoned a merry song,
and the Tzaddik grasped the arm of an old peasant.

"Hey, what is your name?"

"Matiu."

"Come, let's dance, Matiu!"

And the Tzaddik clasped him in his arms and started to dance with him.

Song followed song. The wine drove away the surprise. Slowly the mood became heated up, and by the time the peasants could think over what was happening each one of them was dancing with a Hasid. In the meantime they drained glasses of wine, and the Tzaddik drank with all of them.

"How well you know our songs!" said old Matiu, overcome with emotion. "May God preserve you!"

"May God preserve you too," answered the Tzaddik. "Do you know that today is Purim?"

The intoxicated peasants did not understand the question. The Tzaddik added:

"A Jewish holiday. Haman wanted to destroy us."

"He deserves to be hanged!" cried the excited Matiu.

"In fact he was hanged," responded the *gabbai*.

Reb Hayyem and his musicians intoned a new song, and the whole company continued to dance.

The merriment lasted until daybreak. When it started to get light, the Tzaddik called the coachmen, and the group of Hasidim set out on the homeward journey. The elated peasants went with them as far as the end of the village. The fresh winds of dawn blew into their heated faces and sobered them up. They turned back with eyes downcast. And the Tzaddik turned to his followers:

"We shall be late getting home. Let us recite the *Shema*."

When they reached home, the Tzaddik said joyously to the believers who crowded around him:

"Many of you were astounded, many of you were apprehensive that you have committed a sin, right? You of course know that according to the Midrash, danger threatened our ancestors in Persia because they ate of the repast of Ahasuerus and drank of his wine. But I tell you that what we did tonight was better than the fasting of Mordecai and Esther in those days, and our Purim greater than the Purim of Mordecai and Esther. For you don't know what the sons of Haman would have done!"

—21—

The Great Conflict

t was for Shavuot, the great holiday of the Revelation of the Torah, that the Sasovers and the Dynovers set the date of settling their great conflict. "Let there be light at long last," said the Sasovers, who could no longer bear to listen to the glorification of "the new Star of Dynov." At last they would be able to convince themselves of everything, to see with their own eyes!

But one has to know that both the Dynovers and the Sasovers actually lived in Rymanow and spent only a few holidays away from their community: these with the Tzaddik of Sasov, those with the Tzaddik of Dynov. And of course all this took place at the time when the "Star of Rymanow" was still hiding somewhere behind the clouds.

Besides, one must also observe that not so very long ago the Dynovers, too, had been Sasovers and only forsook their old master when they "noticed something" in Sasov.

And when from Dynov reports of more and more wonderful things were brought on the wings of rumors . . .

What it was they "noticed" in Sasov cannot really be told
without offending the memory of the great Tzaddik. Anyway, the matter is no longer of any importance, since the
Dynover Tzaddik put everything in order. Only on one
single occasion did the renegade Sasovers tell of their
worries, when before the evening prayer they got em-
broiled in a hot dispute in the synagogue courtyard, and
even then such an uproar was created by the issue that
one must consider it a special mercy of Providence that
only five Sasovers and four Dynovers happened to be
present on the occasion, else the whole world would have
been filled with the scandal.

As it happened, the storms of the scene in the synagogue
courtyard soon subsided, but each time the Dynovers returned from a visit to their Tzaddik they could not tell
enough of the sparkling light of the "new star," which visibly hurt the faithful Sasovers deep in their hearts.

"I myself have heard," one of the Sasovers reported, "and
from no less a person than one who is as reliable as our
Master Moses, and he heard it from Reb Hayyem of Berdichev, to whom once the Tzaddik himself had said that in
the powers of the Dynover the 'Other Side'[1] had a share,
and that in his flame there is a spark that stems directly
from 'That Certain One.'"

"Our Tzaddik has never as yet said anything bad about
the Sasover," answered one of the Dynovers mildly.

---

1. "The Other Side" (*sitra ahra*) is a kabbalistic-Hasidic expression referring to the mystical forces of evil in the world, and "That
Certain One" (*P'lonit*, in feminine) refers to Lilith, the arch-demoness.

"Well, what is it that he does say about him?"

"Come, and you can all hear it!"

Finally all of them decided that for Shavuot they would really go to Dynov. On other occasions they could spend only one or two hours with the Tzaddik of Dynov, but on Shavuot they could sit awake with him all through the night, and would have ample opportunity to hear about everything. Perhaps he would even say something about those doings of the Sasover opponents because of which the Dynovers in general considered them "lightweight." In that case, they thought, they would step forward and save the honor of their master!

On the day before the holiday the news spread from mouth to mouth in Dynov and created great excitement:

"The Sasovers have come! The Sasovers have come!"

The younger ones took pleasure in advance imagining what would happen if the wild Sasovers should, by any chance, dare to provoke an incident. The more sedate tried to smooth the ruffled feathers of the hotbloods:

"One must receive them with honor, must call each one of them up to the reading of the Torah, and at the table seat them right next to the Tzaddik!"

"We are not as jealous as the Sasovers," added another one.

And as for the Sasovers, as soon as they arrived in Dynov they noticed that they were in a world very different from Sasov. The eyes did not blaze with wild fires, but rather looked serenely, with etherealized glances, into the distance, as if they wanted to embrace the whole universe. In the streets they did move about dancing, but paced with serious, festive dignity. And, in general, they spoke little. The Tzaddik himself did not clap hands and did not jubilate in his room, but sat and studied with quiet devotion.

As far as studying was concerned, the Sasovers too admitted that in that respect the Dynover was greater—no wonder, since he did nothing else but study, while the Sasover created worlds.

In the evening, when they went to the synagogue, they noticed that here everything was much more beautifully decorated. The walls all around were covered with green boughs and fragrant lilacs, the almemor was overarched by a high baldachin of branches with roses woven into them, around the Holy Ark as many garlands were strung up as was the number of Torah scrolls inside it, and its curtain was studded full with carnations and jasmines. Also over the head of the Tzaddik there was a canopy of flowers, and the whole synagogue was replete with color and fragrance.

"In Sasov they don't honor the Torah this way," thought one of the Sasovers. And he was almost inclined to go over to the side of the Dynovers.

But when they began to pray, and he saw that the Tzaddik himself stood almost motionless in his place, uttering quietly, almost inaudibly, the words, which from the mouth of the Sasover set the whole world ablaze, he repented his momentary wavering, and definitely settled in his mind that in Sasov there was more life. There everything was more fiery, more intense.

The other Sasovers, too, were enchanted by the quiet inspiration. They stood still in their places, deeply moved, and basked in the embrace of the colors and the scents.

"Yes, after all, here in Dynov everything is more beautiful, more festive," they thought to themselves.

But soon they too repented of the involuntary praise their thoughts accorded to Dynov, and resolved to postpone their final judgment until they experienced the night of vigil they were to spend in the company of the Tzaddik.

"Let us hear what he will say! He surely knows that we are here, and will try to sway us from the Sasover!"

An hour later they all sat around the table of the *Bet haMidrash*, in the faint candlelight. The Tzaddik started to read the first book of the Torah, clearly enunciating each separate word, and the Hasidim, listening attentively, followed him by reading silently. When he reached the end of the first book, he stopped, and spoke:

"There are disparate ways in which one can serve the Almighty. And God, who is present everywhere and in everything, understands all of us. Some are seized with a passion, storms arise in their soul, and make their whole body move, and then each of the limbs rejoices, dances, and sings. For not only the mouth can sing, but all the members of the body. Their song is dance, which breaks forth from the depths of the heart. The limbs dance, gyrate to the tune of the world's prayer, then unite into one great free movement, and the heart feels that it embraces the all, and unites with God. He who does not hear the song of the world's prayer, does not understand these movements, like the deaf person who finds himself among dancers and marvels that some make their fingers run back and forth on tightly stretched cords, and the others jump up and down and twirl and wheel. He does not hear the tune, and does not understand the connection."

"So our Tzaddik is right," whispered one of the Sasovers to his neighbor. And the Tzaddik of Dynov continued:

"And then there are those who stand motionless and

wordless before their Creator. And in that motionlessness is contained everything that cannot be expressed in words. Man feels that he is one with God, that he is part of God, because nothing is outside God. The word, the movement, are but expressions of the thought, and of the feeling which contracts, shrinks, so as to be able to find room within the garb of the word and of the movement. But the garb covers only the surface, and the thought and the feeling are the purest without any garb, without form, without expression, because then they are infinite. We speak by keeping silent, like the sea when it is quiet, like the sky when it is clear, without clouds. It is thus that the whole world speaks in the silence of the night."

The Sasovers listened with wonderment to the words of the Tzaddik, and waited impatiently for the end of the second book, when the Tzaddik spoke again:

"Every Tzaddik has his own particular way. Often they even quarrel with each other about which way is better, and on such occasions also those who stand about and watch put in an opinion without really knowing where those ways lead. Like the people of the court, who, when the masters discussed how to decorate the crown of the king, interfered in the discussion with loud voices, and clamorously joined one or the other, and produced such a confusion that the masters could not understand each other's words. But then the king called out and reproached the boisterous people: 'If the masters engage in an argument, they know why they are doing it—each one of them believes that his way is the best to decorate the crown. But you, what do you want?'"

"The Tzaddik knows what we are thinking," whispered one Sasover to his neighbor.

When the third book was concluded, the Dynover continued:

"Once upon a time a king had a great orchard in the midst of a wilderness, and so as to protect it from the wild beasts he stationed watchmen all around the garden, who during the night would signal to one another. One called, 'Hollaho!' and all the others, one after the other, repeated the cry, 'Hollaho!' The strangers, those who were distant, when they heard the cries thought that the watchmen were quarreling, and that was why they shouted at each other. But the king knew that the watchmen did it only to hear each others' voices. And woe to the orchard if one of the watchmen dies, and his companion cries in vain 'Hollaho! Hollaho!'"

All the men sitting around the table understood the reference, and knew what the Tzaddik was speaking about. The Sasovers huddled together and looked with ecstasy at the face of the Tzaddik.

After the fourth book the Tzaddik spoke even more clearly:

"There are those who, when a burglar surprises them at night, instantly raise a big noise and drive him away. But this shows timidity. The stouthearted waits until the burglar enters, and attacks him only after he has broken into the house and grabbed something to steal; thus, if he delivers him to the law, he gets rid of him once and for all. One Tzaddik, as soon as he senses the approach of the Evil One, instantly chases him away. Another will seemingly give in to the temptation, and subdues the Evil One only when it has already taken something from him, and thus also changes the evil into good."

The Sasovers looked at each other amazed: the Tzaddik

spoke in favor of his great opponent! For it was evident to all of them that he was alluding to the "light" things of the Tzaddik of Sasov.

When they finished the Five Books of the Torah, the Tzaddik of Dynov said only this:

"You know, do you not, that God, the Torah, and Israel are one. One Tzaddik devotes himself only to the Torah, and thus serves God, another only to Israel, and, perhaps, that is an even higher degree."

And everybody knew that he was again alluding to the Tzaddik of Sasov, who was not as great as he in learning, but was great in leading Israel.

When the light of dawn poured into the half-dark *Bet haMidrash*, almost all the candles had been burnt down, and only a few followers still drowsed around the table. And at the head, next to the Tzaddik, sat the nine visitors from Sasov, five to his right and four to his left. Only they were still awake, and studied the Book of *Zohar*, listening in the meantime to the explanations of the Tzaddik. They were no longer angry at him. But still, a full reconciliation was effected only when the "great star" arose in Rymanow, and people came to him from both Sasov and Dynov to celebrate the holidays.

——22——

The Cow of Reb Dovedl

t was a rainy, dark autumn night, and precisely the night of Wednesday, when people are being frightened by evil spirits and wandering ghosts. The sad news spread from house to house:

"The cow of Reb Dovedl is dying."

"May the Almighty have compassion," added everybody who passed on the unhappy news.

The rain washed the dark village, and the wind whined, as if it were a wandering soul awaiting purification. But the people knew only one thing: the cow of Reb Dovedl was dying!

For nine years the poor Reb Dovedl laid aside penny after penny, for nine years he carried in the very bottom of his heart the great dream that he would feed his children with his own cattle, would provide them with milk, butter, and cheese, and would no longer need the quart of milk the rich Reb Khezkel was sending him every Sabbath. Then his children, too, would be able to have coffee for breakfast every day, just like the children of Reb Zelig, and then their faces too would be full and ruddy-cheeked.

It was with this beautiful dream that he quieted himself down on the occasions when he jumped up from his place with a discomposed countenance, and cried with a hoarse voice:

"These two louts will be the death of me!"

The two louts were always two different boys. Once they were the children of Reb Khezkel, once those of Reb Mayshe. Reb Dovedl implanted into their hearts the words of the Holy Torah, and often his soul rejoiced when he saw that his pupils so nicely broadened their knowledge of the Law.

On such occasions he stroked his long black beard with satisfaction and was proud of his vocation. After all, to give instruction in the Holy Torah was superior to teaching that Paris was a city, Pata a village, the Danube a river, or that the cat had four feet and the chicken two. At other times, however, Reb Dovedl did not see his profession as such a splendid work and walked up and down the small House of Study fulminating and furious. But then he remembered that only a few more florins were lacking until the realization of his dream, and continued to sell his sick lungs for a few more florins.

Often the halter of the cow was almost there in his hands, but something always intervened, and Reb Dovedl dropped the ropes. In the meantime the little children grew up, and his house was filled with new blessings. Nine years passed in this manner, until at long last he was able to go to the fair and return with a beautiful, big, speckled cow. He himself led the precious animal, and on the way home collected the scraps of straw littering the wayside, as if to prove in advance to the guest that it would suffer no want in his house. He reached his home covered with sweat and dust, but with a face shining with joy, and tied the cow to the big nut tree. His children hung about the newcomer all day long and tried to please it as best they could. The whole village spoke of Reb Dovedl's cow as of the luck of the poor man of the fairy tale.

And three days later the sad news spread from house to house:

"Reb Dovedl's cow is dying!"

Who could tell what had happened to the innocent animal? The very day after its arrival it became sick. Reb Dovedl tried to take care of it as best he could, he fondled it, caressed it, incessantly asked it what was the trouble, was it better; but the cow did not respond, it only looked at him with its big eyes, and kept silent.

The agony of the cow lasted several days, until finally, on Friday toward evening, when the Sabbath rest descended on the earth, when in the rooms the festive candles were lit, the poor animal gave up its soul.

For Reb Dovedl the Sabbath candles seemed to be sad mourning lights. But he soon collected himself, covered the dead cow with a big canvas, put on his festive clothes, and hurried to the synagogue.

The little village synagogue too wore festive garb. And Reb Dovedl stood before the flaming tapers, and sang with devotion the Psalm about "the redeemed of the Lord," the pious, whom God "blesseth so that they are multiplied greatly, and suffereth not their cattle to decrease. . . ."

When Queen Sabbath, who brings into every house light
and joy, departed, the people of the village gathered in the
house of Reb Dovedl for the "farewell meal of the Queen."
Every one of them took along the remainders of the "three
royal repasts," and they all enjoyed the dishes, singing
sacred songs in between. At the end of the farewell repast,
Reb Dovedl, who on those occasions used to entertain his
audience with sacred stories, embarked on one this time
too, as if wishing to soothe everybody, even though he was
not as merry as was his wont to be at other farewell gath-
erings in honor of the Queen. This is what he said:

Once the Baal Shem—may his memory be blessed—
stopped at an inn, where the tavern keeper happened to
be engaged in sorting out his papers. The Baal Shem sat
down at the table, told the host to continue his work, and
asked him to allow him too to have a glance at what he
was doing. The innkeeper readily acceded to the Tzaddik's
request. At that moment an old piece of writing came into
his hands, and the Baal Shem asked him what kind of a
paper it was.

"An old, valueless promissory note," answered the innkeeper.

"And is there still any chance that you can receive the
amount mentioned in it?" asked the Baal Shem.

"None at all," answered the host. "The poor man died a
long time ago and left behind no heirs."

"If so, would you let me have this note?" asked the Tzaddik.

The innkeeper folded up the paper and gave it to him.
The Baal Shem right away held the paper over the burning candle, and in a moment the note went up in flames

and turned into ashes. A few moments later the innkeeper's coachman came into the room and told his master that the white horse in the stable had suddenly collapsed and died.

The innkeeper wanted to rush out to see for himself, but the Baal Shem caught him by his arm and said to him:

"Know that in that animal dwelt the soul of your debtor, who was sentenced to repaying you his old debt by working for you. But now that you have forgiven the debt and presented the note to me, the soul that had transmigrated into the animal became liberated."

Reb Khezkel remarked jokingly:

"Who knows what soul was liberated from the cow of Reb Dovedl?"

But Reb Dovedl replied seriously:

"It is not seemly to joke about such things. Nobody can know whether his soul did not return to this world in order to pay off a debt incurred in a previous life. After all, you know the story of the wandering soul of the evil brother."

A shudder went through Reb Khezkel. Who knows, he thought, perhaps he too was such an evil brother, and by sending a quart of milk every week to Reb Dovedl he was repaying a debt to him, who perhaps was his brother in that other life. And he resolved then and there that he would from then on send him that quart of milk every day.

And Reb Dovedl, as if he had sensed the blessing that descended upon him from Reb Khezkel, became merrier and more loquacious. He continued to tell much more about wandering souls. He told about that big black dog that appeared while the Baal Shem was praying and disappeared immediately thereafter. He told about the bride

and groom whom the Baal Shem joined in marriage, and
the bride died right there under the baldachin, and the Baal
Shem comforted the heart-stricken relatives: "Know that
they were engaged to be married in a previous life, but left
each other, and they had to come back to the world only
in order to fulfill their promise that they had broken in
that life; now, with this wedding this was done, and thus
the souls of both of them could be liberated."

And Reb Dovedl told many more stories with which he
wanted to prove, not so much to his guests, as to himself,
that behind every occurrence that to the feeble human eyes
seemed unintelligible or unjust there was concealed the
secret of some wandering soul.

The hour became late, and Reb Dovedl took also the
Zohar explanation, which pertains to the farewell feast of
the Queen, from the mysterious world of the wandering
souls:

Scripture says, "These are the laws." The *Zohar* adds:
"This is the secret of the wandering of souls. . . ." The Rebbe
of Mezhirech—may his memory be blessed—once asked
the Baal Shem, what was the explanation of this? And the
Tzaddik told him to go out into the forest, wait there for
an hour on the banks of the brook under the big poplar,
but remain silent, utter not a single word. The Mezhirecher
went and settled down at the designated spot. Suddenly
he saw that on the opposite bank of the brook a wanderer
arrived, sat down under a tree, rested for half an hour, then
got up and went away. But his purse fell out of his pocket
and remained where he had sat. Soon another wayfarer
came, sat down in the same place, noticed the ownerless
purse, picked it up, and hurried away with it. Then a third

journeyer arrived. He too settled down under the tree and soon fell asleep. Half an hour later the first wanderer came back, looking for his lost purse. When he saw the sleeper, he became suspicious of him, shook him awake, and when the man insisted that he knew nothing, the first wanderer got enraged, administered the third man a thorough beating, and then went away. The Mezhirecher observed the happenings and marveled, but understood nothing: where was the connection, and why did he have to witness the events? When he returned and told the Baal Shem what he had seen, the Baal Shem said:

"Know, that in the previous life the first wayfarer owed the second one as much money as there was in the purse, but he denied it. The third wanderer was the judge, who did not take enough trouble to discover the truth, and thoughtlessly pronounced him not guilty. Therefore the powers in heaven resolved that all three of them had to return to the world. Now justice has been restored: the second wanderer got his money back, and the third one, who passed the heedless judgment, got his beating. This is why the *Zohar* says, "the Baal Shem concluded, "'These are the laws.' . . . 'This is the secret of the wandering of the souls.'"

When, about midnight, the farewell repast of the Queen ended, Reb Dovedl accompanied his guests across his courtyard. And as they passed the covered body of the mysterious cow, they all looked at it, and it seemed to all of them as if over the black canvas there hovered the liberated soul, waiting for next day's funeral.

——23——

Good-bye to the Booth

n the eighth day of the Feast of Booths the Tzaddik of Blazowa would not leave the festive booth even for a moment. All through the eight days he sated the hunger of his body and his soul in the booth. There he delved, together with his followers, into the secrets of the Torah and the mysteries of the prayers, and there he put down his head to rest when sleep overpowered him. Only toward the evening would he leave the booth for an hour or so, to delight in the works of the Creator out there in the open, in the meadows, fields, and forests. But throughout the last day, like a lovesick bridegroom who wants to spend every minute with his bride before taking leave of her, he sat in the booth, all transfigured, and gazed intoxicated at the decorations hanging from the walls and the ceiling, as if they were the jewels and earrings of the beautiful Bride that enchant the eye and fill the soul with pleasure.

213

The gray canvas walls were covered with snow-white draperies, upon which verses from the Psalms, surrounded by big multicolored garlands, created a sumptuous festoonery. In the middle, home-woven carpets represented scenes from the messianic days as described by the prophets: a curly wooled lamb was grazing together with a wolf in a grassy field, a lion and a fawn both bent their heads over the hay of the manger, a little boy was leading a tiger, and in front of his feet a viper lay peacefully. In the center of stars carved into wood and covered with shining silver there glistened in gold the names of the sacred spiritual guests of the booth: Abraham, Isaac, Jacob, Moses, Aaron, Joseph, and David. Overhead, the fragrant roofing of green pine and oak branches was crisscrossed by colorful paper chains, which combined to form big David's Stars, with flowers and fruits from the Holy Land and small bottles full of oil from Hebron, wine from Carmel, and date-honey from Sharon hanging down from their corners.

The Tzaddik imbibed the heady fragrance of the booth. The happy cup of his intoxicated soul ran over, and he suddenly turned to his followers:

"This, my brothers, is the most wonderful, most sacred act. All year round the Children of Israel are driven by worry, sorrow, and suffering, and in vain do we try to rise up into the Heights, in vain does our soul strive to reach the heavenly summits. The weight of the worries weighs heavily on us, the mire of sorrow bespatters the festive garb of our soul, and the sufferings alienate the heart from its God. For a moment, a minute, an hour we do rise up on the wings of a sacred act. Morning comes, and we tie the *tefillin* around our arm and feel as if our arm had become liberated from the chains of everyday work, and as if our hand were connected with the Heights and could rise and hover in the infinite; but the weight of our bodies presses upon it and pulls us down to the earth, many times into the mire. And when we tie the word of God to our foreheads we feel that we consecrate our heads and our thoughts to the Creator of the world, and we are happy that rays from the heights of the spheres flash into our eyes, and connect us with the eternal source of lights of the Highest Thought. But the demons of evil thoughts come, and tear us away by force, and carry us back into the realm of the body, the bread, the craving. Only for a moment can a sacred act elevate a member of our body. But on the Feast of Booths we enter with our entire body into the sacred act, the sacred air of the booth surrounds, embraces, and sanctifies our whole body, each and every one of our limbs."

"This is the mystery of the Holy Booth," thought the believers enthusiastically. And the Tzaddik continued:

"If we let our eyes roam about in the booth, we see that its walls are wobbling canvas, which the wind dents in and puffs up as the sail of a ship. Should it so wish, it could pick up the whole booth, and whisk it away into the infinite, the nothing. We look up into the Heights, and perceive that our cover consists of fading boughs, falling branches, through which rain and sunshine can penetrate. And even though we entrust the sails of our lives to the wings of storms, we nevertheless feel that the wings of the Creator hover over us, and the Shekhinah covers us with her sacred protection. The Master of the Universe is our booth, and His booth is a safer refuge than all the bastioned castles and palaces of the earth."

"May the Merciful One build up the crumbling tent of

David!" a deep voice suddenly broke in with a sigh. The followers pricked up their ears, but quickly returned to listening to the words of the Tzaddik, who continued with his eyes shut:

"And if we shut our eyes, behold, we see that in response to our words of invitation there come the ancestral spirits to visit the booth, the seven shepherds, the forefathers, who, while wandering in deserts, saw God in sacred visions. Moses, who brought the eternal Law out of fire and flame on Mount Sinai shaking with thunder and lightning, and Aaron, in the high priestly robe of the Holy of Holies, and Joseph, and David in royal splendor, with crown and harp. Come, supernal visitors, come, sacred guests, we invite you. And they do come, and we know with humble pride that they are ours, the royal ancestors of those who dwell in booths, and nobody can take them away from us. And many thousands of years convene in the depths of the booth, many millennia which are ours, many millennia of hurts and humiliations, but also of prophets and martyrs, many millennia of waves and chasms, but also of pearls and lighthouses."

Outside, the sun was setting. Red rays filtered through the crevices of the ceiling's boughs into the gloom of the booth. The golden names of the patriarchs and kings carved into the ornamental stars glittered in the dark.

"The time of the evening prayer has arrived," said the Tzaddik dreamily. "We must take leave of the booth."

"Let us join hands," could suddenly be heard from several lips. In a moment the hands of the believers joined in a strong chain around the Tzaddik, who for a moment remained standing motionless in the middle of the circle, and then, looking about sadly, said:

"When the bridegroom takes leave of his bride, he covers the sadness of his heart with the gaiety of his face, lest the sorrow of the bride increase. The Shekhinah avoids places of sorrow. Let us take leave of the booth with dance, my brothers."

The song of a Psalm resounded on the lips of the believers, and the silver-headed Tzaddik started to dance to its melody in the growing twilight of the booth. Wherever he turned with his outstretched arms and his soft steps, the chain quickly opened up for him, and once his steps moved away, it again closed up and surged ahead, as if the chain of the hands were also swaying to and fro following the rhythm of the song, like the reverberating waves after the ship dancing next to the shore. The whole rocking movement was almost unconscious, and the believers barely noticed that the Tzaddik stopped in the middle of the circle and, wrapped in thought, contemplated the embroidered scenes on the carpets of the booth; as if the messianic days, the time of eternal peace, had come to life before him, with the curly wooled lamb grazing together with the wolf in a grassy field, the lion and the fawn both bending their heads over the hay of the manger, and a little boy leading the tiger, and in front of his feet a viper lying peacefully. Visions of the prophets swarmed before his eyes, came to life on the walls of the booth. No bastion would be needed, no towering fort, the booth of the Lord would protect everybody.

When the first evening stars shone through the boughs of the booth's ceiling, the Tzaddik sadly started to leave. At the door he turned around, and, surrounded by his followers, he walked backward for a while so that his eyes should see the festive booth a little longer. His lips murmured a Psalm, as if he wanted to send a last few soft words of farewell to the booth. Then he turned, and with quick steps hurried to the synagogue, which was sparkling in festive light. With his thoughts fixed on the booth, he recited the evening prayer:

"O spread over us the tent of Your peace."

And the followers too recited sadly the prayer:

"Blessed be He who spreads the tent of peace over us, and over all Israel, and over Jerusalem."

——24——

Three Bursts of Laughter

e who has not seen a Friday evening at the Tzaddik of Nemirov has never seen real joy. Wonders, it is true, were being told also about the Friday evenings of Berdichev, but the initiate knew that the powers of the Tzaddik of Berdichev were greater on any day of the week than on the Sabbath, even though they also knew that this diminishing of powers stemmed precisely from his inability to restrain the flames breaking forth from his soul. For as soon as Friday dawned, the presentiment of the Sabbath began to take hold of him, and the nearer the holy day came the more he was overpowered by rejoicing and jubilation, which soon reached their highest degree, so that when dusk came and it was time to greet Queen Sabbath the great blaze had exhausted his strength to the point of being able to step before the countenance of the Queen only with a languid heart.

In contrast to this, the Tzaddik of Nemirov was past master at curbing the flames. The evil tongues, and especially the Berdichevers, even scoffed at him for this ability, and said that the greatest miracle performed by the Nemirover was that once, when he wanted to have a look at Gehenna, as soon as he entered, it cooled down. But those who had seen the Friday evening at Nemirov even one single time would become convinced that his coolness was rather dignity, the dignity of a king who has a deep passion for his queen, is attached with love to his people, but nevertheless remains dignified. And he to whom it was granted to spend one Sabbath of his life in Nemirov could see that on Friday afternoon, when the Tzaddik came out of the bath, his face was white like the moon in winter, his eyes shone as they glanced into the distance, and big drops of water glittered on his long white beard, those drops of water which in the heavenly balance fall into the scale of good deeds and often decide the fate of the whole world.

The Tzaddik approached the synagogue with slow, stately steps, and only when his eyes glimpsed the light of the candles burning in honor of the Sabbath did the restrained fire of enthusiasm break forth from his heart. He entered the synagogue almost running, went straight up to the Holy Ark, and began to recite the prayers.

Who could describe that prayer? That welcoming of the Sabbath!?

And when the prayers were concluded, the believers gathered in the Tzaddik's home. The table was set in a big room for all those who had come from all parts of the world to spend a Sabbath in Nemirov. But also the locals did come, having partaken of the first meal of the Sabbath in their own homes with their families, and then they hurried to the Tzaddik to listen to his *Kiddush.*

The room was full of believers with expectant, radiant faces, and all eyes were turned to the back door through which they expected the Tzaddik to come out of his room where he would be locked in, immersed in kabbalistic mysteries.

Suddenly a deep silence enveloped the gathering. The crowd of followers made room for the Tzaddik, clad in a white silk robe. His whole being smiled, and his happy smiles embraced all those who filled the room. And it seemed that from that smile everything was miraculously transformed. The room became bigger, more spacious, the ceiling higher, the worn walls became as if transformed into marble, and through the open door of the marble palace Queen Sabbath herself entered, accompanied by white angels, and stopped before the white throne of the Tzaddik. And the white angels hovered about the believers, placed a sparkling crown on the head of each one of them, and breathed the Sabbath soul into them.

The Tzaddik looked around with smiling eyes, and then intoned the Sabbath song, and the believers sang with him. The Tzaddik burned, clapped his hands, exulted, danced; but even then he did not lose his dignity, although in his enthusiasm he was often exposed to the temptation of taking Queen Sabbath to dance and offending the dignity of the royal Bride.

Such was an ordinary Friday evening in Nemirov. Let alone when some extraordinary event came to pass! And such extraordinary events were not even so very rare, even though the following occurrence belonged among the more conspicuous ones, and the Berdichevers don't want to believe it to this day.

One Friday evening the Tzaddik of Nemirov sat at the table sadly. His eyes gazed gloomily, and his whole body was rigid. Nobody knew why the Rebbe was sad, why he did not smile as was his wont, why he did not embrace the believers with his smile, so that the joy of Sabbath, the jubilation of Sabbath, should spread all about. But who would dare to disturb the reverie of the Tzaddik! If he looks up into the Heights, surely great things are taking place there, and if he is sad he has good reason for it. The sadness of the Tzaddik affected the believers. All of them were overcome by a mute despondency, and their troubled eyes searched the Tzaddik's somber features.

What could be happening? What will become of the world?

Suddenly a flutter crossed the face of the Tzaddik, his eyes began to twinkle, and a long, sweet laughter burst forth from his lips. Then his face clouded over again, but only for a few moments, which were followed by another outburst of sweet laughter, and this was repeated a third time.

After the third laughter a radiant joy settled on the countenance of the Tzaddik, and he intoned, smiling, a new Sabbath song. The believers sang with him, even though, while singing, they often wondered, what could the three laughters have meant? That weighty things had to lie behind them, that much was clear to everybody. But who is so daring as to ask, when the whole world knows that nothing annoys the Tzaddik of Nemirov as much as curiosity!

But at the outgoing of the Sabbath the answer came of itself.

They were in the midst of bidding farewell to Queen Sabbath with sad songs, when the Tzaddik suddenly called out:

"Mendele tailor, come here!"

A shriveled little old man approached the Tzaddik, and remained standing before him with downcast eyes.

"What did you do, Mendele, Friday evening?"

Mendele did not answer. He only stood there with downcast eyes and blushing cheeks.

"Tell us, Mendele," the Tzaddik urged him on. "You don't have to be ashamed."

And Mendele, eyes downcast and cheeks blushing, related with much hemming and hawing that he had lived all his life on the work of his hands, but that recently, having reached old age, his income had been dwindling, and for several weeks now he was forced to sell something of his household furnishings in order to be able to buy candles and *hallah* for the Sabbath. This week, however, nothing more was left in his house to sell. He did not want to beg, to panhandle, and therefore decided rather to fast on the Sabbath as well, to stay in the synagogue after the Friday evening services, and to spend the night there in prayer until the morning, when the believers would return. But his heart gave him no rest, and, in addition, he was afraid lest people notice that he stayed in the synagogue overnight, and, learning the reason, would send him the requisites of the Sabbath. Hence he resolved to go home, after all, even if he had to stay in the dark in his house. But when he entered his room he saw with surprise that candles were burning on the table, on the white tablecloth rested two *hallahs*, and next to them wine, fish, and meat. At first he was not happy with what he saw, because he thought that his wife had accepted donations from somebody. But she told him that she had bought everything with the money she got for her wedding ring, which had got lost soon after their wedding, and now she had found it again, almost miraculously. He was seized with such an overpowering happiness that he simply could not control himself. He had the wonderful feeling that this was his wedding day, and in his jubilant joy, while singing Sabbath songs, he got hold of his hoary-headed wife, and started to dance with her. And they danced three times around in the little, narrow garret chamber.

While telling the last part of his story Mendele cast down his eyes even more. The Tzaddik smiled. And the believers knew why he had laughed three times on Friday evening.

Turning serious, the Tzaddik remarked:

"Dreadful calamities were in the making. The heavenly accuser gathered terrible charges against Israel, and the Shekhinah was looking down on earth with flashing anger. But then she saw the hoary-headed couple dance in their Sabbath joy and began to smile. The Shekhinah smiled three times, and those three smiles decided the fate of the Children of Israel."

And the believers also knew why the Tzaddik had been so sad before the three laughters.

---25---

God, If You Had a Flock . . .

an you hear the ringing of the sheep bells, Meir?" asked the Baal Shem, turning back to his perspiring skinny disciple, who followed the Master respectfully at a distance of three steps, in his climb upward in the thick of the forest.

"I can hear nothing," answered the disciple, "only the song of the birds, the buzzing of the wasps, the flutter of the butterflies."

"That too is a service of God," said the Baal Shem. "But I can already hear also the ringing of the sheep bells. Soon we shall reach the summit."

They broke a path for themselves through the closely twined trees and bushes. The rays of the sun flickered through the thicket, and under the steps of the master and the disciple the dry leaves crunched and cracked. In the distance a startled fawn ran, then stopped and froze. A

225

silent breeze wafted light fragrances. Their breathing became more and more labored.

"Do you know which is the Verse of the Bird in the Chapter of Songs?" the Baal Shem suddenly asked his disciple.

The youth with the ascetic face looked at his Master with flashing eyes. In his radiant look there was the answer: how could he not know the Chapter of Songs? He rapidly recited:

"Yea, the sparrow hath found a house, and the swallow a nest for herself, where she may lay her young—Thine altars, O Lord of Hosts, my King and my God."

"If you say it so rapidly," said the Baal Shem gently, "it is no longer a song. You know the text, but do you understand its meaning? Do you hear how the bird sings in the tree? Quietly, full of happiness and confidence, and its joyful melody is carried everywhere by the wind. And do you know the Song of the Wind?"

Meir now quoted slowly, rhythmically, from the Chapter of Songs:

"I will say to the north, 'Give up!' and to the south, 'Keep not back, bring My sons from far, and My daughters from the end of the earth.'"

"Everything sings only of this, only of this," repeated the Baal Shem. "The bird, the fawn, the wind, the sun."

The air seemed to become lighter, thinner, and the breeze seemed to waft toward them fresher and fresher fragrances of spices. They reached the summit. A broad clearing spread before them. Suddenly, the horizon opened up before their eyes. All about rose the chains of the Polish mountains. Beneath them lay small villages, scattered farmsteads, with low huts. Around the edges of the clearing, fragrant with wild thyme, a woolly flock of sheep was grazing, kept together by stout bellwethers. In the middle, at the foot of a rock, next to a gurgling spring, a gaunt youth was dancing, flailing in the air with his big shepherd's crook. He kept his tressy head turned upward and sang aloud, repeating the words again and again:

> God, if You had a flock,
> I would graze it for nothing,
> I would watch it for nothing.

With eyes raised to heaven he danced around the rock, the spring, then jumped back and forth across the ditch next to him and cried more and more loudly and excitedly:

> I do it for You, Lord of the World,
> I do it for You, Lord of the World.

"Look at that shepherd," said the Baal Shem to his disciple, pointing with his finger. "You see, his service of God stands on a higher grade than that of all of us. With his pure flame he breaks through the windows of the heavens. This man has the name of Moses, perhaps also the soul of Moses. He could be the redeemer of the world."

"Let us go nearer to him," said Meir, with eyes burning with curiosity.

The dancing shepherd did not even notice the approach of the two strangers. The Baal Shem addressed him gently:

"I would like to talk to you, shepherd Moses."

"I am a day laborer, and my time belongs to my master," was the curt answer.

"Only for a few minutes," begged the Baal Shem.

"Every minute of mine belongs to him."

"And when you dance and jump?"

"That I am doing for the Lord of the World. That is permitted."

"I too want to talk to you about the Lord of the World."

The shepherd gazed at him with his big dark eyes. Then he raised his crook, and began again to sing and jump, and sang loudly, passionately:

> God, if You had a flock,
> I would graze it for nothing.

When he stopped for a moment, the Baal Shem grabbed him by the arm, and drove his glance deep into his eyes:

"Come with me to the big spring! There I shall talk to you about the Lord of the World."

The shepherd obeyed, as if the rays from the Baal Shem's eyes had fettered him. He lowered his crook, and quietly followed the Master to the other side of the clearing. The Baal Shem took hold of his hand and said:

"Know then, shepherd Moses, that the Lord of the World is in exile."

"Why? How?" cried the shepherd, appalled. He tore his hand out of that of the Baal Shem, and clenched his fist.

"Because His children are in exile. Come with me to the big spring, and we shall immerse ourselves in its clear waters."

"I do that every day."

"But now you will do it for the redemption of the Lord of the World. And you will say a blessing over it."

"I do not know how to say a blessing."

"You will say it after me."

The shepherd followed the Baal Shem as if in a daze. When they reached the spring, they submerged in its waters three times. The rays of the sun quickly dried the drops of water on their bodies, and then all three sat down around the spring in whose smooth mirror the firmament was reflected in blue purity, and in it the images of the three seekers of heavenly secrets.

"Open the Gates of Heaven!" the Baal Shem said to his disciple.

The shepherd gave a start, expecting heavenly miracles. The Baal Shem pointed to the bulky prayer book.

"Do you know the sacred letter?"

"There was nobody to teach me letters."

"Listen then well, O shepherd! Meir will read the order of the Three Vigils, and I shall tell it to you in your language."

The words purled quietly, sadly, as they sat next to the pure spring:

"'A voice is heard in the Height, lamentation and bitter weeping.' When the Sanctuary was destroyed, a voice came and awakened the fathers in their graves: 'Fathers of the World! You are slumbering in your graves, and do not know that your children went into exile, with their hands tied at their back, a millstone around their neck. Wake up, get up!'

"The first to rise was Abraham, stricken in years, and he cried: 'Lord of the World! You know that I walked the way of truth before You. You tested me ten times, and I stood all ten tests—where are my children? I cannot hear their voices on this earth which You promised us with a sacred oath.' And the Holy One, blessed be His name, answers: 'Abraham, Abraham, friend of My soul, they forsook the sacred covenant and served idols!' 'If so, let them be blotted out, for the sake of Your Holy Name!'"

"Abraham was right," said the shepherd.

The Baal Shem pierced him with his eyes.

"This is how all the Fathers and Mothers spoke. Only Rachel raised her voice in bitter lamentation. 'How did my children sin against You? They placed an idol into Your house, a rival? I endured more, much more. When Jacob served seven years for me, in his great love of me, he gave me a secret sign so that my father, Laban, should not be able to deceive him. But when I saw that at night my father sent Leah into the tent of Jacob, I gave the secret sign to my sister so that she should not be humiliated. I brought a rival into my home, and I overcame my jealousy. And You, Lord of the World, are jealous of a graven image and cannot forgive?'"

"Rachel was right," interrupted the shepherd excitedly.

"And Rachel cried, and sobbed, and could not be comforted. And the Shekhinah too raised her voice and cried together with her. And sixty times ten thousand heavenly angels too woke up and cried with her. And the crying could be heard in the Highest Heavens, and seven hundred times a thousand secret worlds trembled. And the Lord God too cried in His Concealment, as it is written."

A tremor seized the shepherd, his eyes filled with tears, and he cried aloud. The Baal Shem looked at him with commiseration and continued from the Chapter of Radiance:

"Rabbi Simeon cried and said: 'Woe that the exile lasts thus long, and who can endure it? When the Holy One, blessed be He, delivered Israel into the hands of that ser-

vant, into the dominion of Edom, He called together all
the Hosts of Heaven, and called the archangel Gabriel, who
has a scribe's pen in his girdle, and said: Hold back the
sentence until I bewail My children. Let Me mourn over
them and do not try to comfort Me, O Heavenly Hosts.
And He cleaved clefts and fissures into heavens, and said:
My children, my dear children, I am calling the four winds
of the world and am saying to them: East, East, South,
South, if My children come to you, look at their faces, see
how they became changed, and how they became black-
ened by suffering. North, North, West, West, have mercy
on them and protect them. My children, My children, O
what did I do to you! I passed a sentence, but you and I
are together going into exile. Moses, my faithful shepherd,
why did you not watch over My children, the sacred flock,
which I delivered into your hand?'"

"Moses should have taken care of the flock," interrupted
the shepherd excitedly.

"Now the Lord of the World too wanders with us. The
Shekhinah is in exile. Did you hear, shepherd? Listen to
the rest of the order of the Three Vigils.

"The Holy One, blessed be He, said to Rachel: 'My daughter, My sister, My shepherdess, My only one, who are spread-
ing your wings toward the four winds of the world, I beg
you, go with them, remain with our children, so as to protect them in the four corners of the world.' And Rachel
answered: 'Lord of the World, I will not go, so that I see
not how Your enemies destroy my children, and You have
forgotten us and left us there among them.' And the Holy
One, blessed be He, answered: 'I shall redeem and resur-
rect Israel, as it is written, "Refrain thy voice from weep-

ing, and thine eyes from tears . . . for thy children shall return to their own border.""""

The shepherd sat in his place, in an almost unconscious self-absorption, and watched the mirror image of the growing dusk, and the cooling, growing sun disk, as reflected in the water of the spring. Suddenly he was awakened from his reverie by the alarming call of the Baal Shem:

"Shepherd Moses, do you want to redeem the Lord of the World out of His exile?"

"What can ignorant me do?" answered the shepherd sadly.

"If you ask, you are powerless. But if you want it, the great fulfillment is yours. The pure will of a pure man can bring redemption."

"I am only a simple shepherd."

"Rachel too was a shepherd girl, who watched over the sheep of her father and waited for what was destined for her and became the mother of Israel. Shepherd Moses, rise, and say that you want the redemption—that you want to watch for nothing the flock of God, as you have said in song and dance there around the rock and the ditch. Do you want it?"

The shepherd suddenly jumped up, raised his crook, and shouted at the top of his voice:

"I do want it! I do want it!"

At that moment the booming, sharp peal of bells from the valley broke into the silence, and on the mountain a nervous, wheezing tingle became its echo. The Baal Shem rose, and the disciple followed him, trembling. Down in the valley, from the edge of the village, one could see red tongues of fire quiver and flicker and rise and paint the

horizon purple with a frightening rapidity. Over the small houses sparks flew, and the bells of the church tower spread their mournful warning all about. One by one the bells of the other villages responded, and the sounds mixed together, the deep ones and the high ones, the booming and the tinkling. Up on the mountain the flock scattered, frightened, the sheep ran to and fro, bleating, their bells ringing.

"My flock!" cried the shepherd in desperation. "The evening is coming! They must be led back to their fold! My flock!"

He tore his hands away from the Baal Shem, started running, and with a few leaps he was back at the clearing, on top of the rock.

The Baal Shem looked after him with pain. The shepherd stood there on the rock in the gathering dusk. The glory of the last sunrays crowned his head. He raised his two palms to his mouth and through them he let out a long, wistful whistle, which sounded as if it were the drawn-out sound of the *shofar*. From all around, from the forest and the dense bushes, the sheep came in response to his call, with bells ringing, in groups, one by one, and gathered around the shepherd.

The Baal Shem watched the scene as if enchanted. He knew that the fire, the alarm of the church bells, was the work of satanic powers, so that the redemption should not be realized. Its time had not yet come. But when he looked up and saw the purple of heaven, which was full of fissures and shreds, as if the King had torn His purple robe in His pain over the loss of His son, his heart filled with mercy, and he prayed:

"Lord of the World! Look down upon this simple creature of Yours, who loves You so much and loves his flock so much. With one whistle call he can gather his scattered sheep. Fulfill the word of Your prophet, O Lord, and gather Your scattered flock from the corners of the world, as You have promised, 'I shall whistle for them and gather them.'"

Joseph Patai

Joseph Patai was a Hungarian Jewish poet, author, translator, editor, lecturer, and Zionist leader. For close to four decades (until his *aliyah* to Palestine in 1939) he was the foremost exponent, representative, and propagator of Jewish culture in Hungary. His monthly, *Mult és Jövő* (Past and Future), was recognized as the most beautifully produced Jewish periodical in Europe and the most influential factor in Jewish cultural life in Hungary. His translations into Hungarian of the Hebrew poets of all ages (published in five volumes) were acclaimed as a masterly contribution to Hungarian poetry. Under his chairmanship the Pro Palestine Association of Hungarian Jews became the center in Hungary of support for the economic, social, and cultural development of the *Yishuv*. His biography of Theodor Herzl (published also in Hebrew, German, and English translations) was the first full-size study of the founder of Zionism, who was born and grew up in Budapest. His Hasidic stories, written in Hungarian and presented in this volume in an English translation, are a rare poetic re-creation of a world that is no more.

Raphael Patai

Raphael Patai, the son of Joseph Patai, was born and grew up in Budapest. An internationally known anthropologist, biblical scholar, and cultural historian, he is the author of more than thirty books, which were translated into ten languages and widely acclaimed for their originality. They include *Israel Between East and West, Hebrew Myths* (with Robert Graves), *The Hebrew Goddess, The Arab Mind, The Jewish Mind, Myth and Modern Man, Tents of Jacob, Jewish Race* (with Jennifer Patai), *Gates to the Old City, The Messiah Texts, On Jewish Folklore, Robert Graves and the Hebrew Myths, The Seed of Abraham, Apprentice in Budapest, Between Budapest and Jerusalem, Journeyman in Jerusalem,* and *The Jewish Alchemists.* He lived in Jerusalem from 1933 to 1947, earned the first Ph.D. degree to be awarded by the Hebrew University of that city, founded and headed the Palestine Institute of Folklore and Ethnology, and after 1947 taught at various American universities.